MONICA

Graham Loveluck-Edwards

ISBN: 978-1-915439-88-8

Printed and bound in the UK by
Severn, Ashville Industrial Estate, Bristol Road, Gloucester, GL2 5EU

Published by:
Candy Jar Books
Mackintosh House
136 Newport Road
Cardiff, CF24 1DJ
www.candyjarbooks.co.uk

Dedicated to the loving memory of Jeanne (aka Jasia or Jan),
whose stories, words and memories have been captured in this book

RÉPUBLIQUE FRANÇAISE

RÉPUBLIQUE FRANÇAISE

Recensement
5/1944
S.A.L.

NON TRAVAILLE

CARTE D'IDENTITÉ
D'ÉTRANGER
N°[illegible]

Nom:

N°8515[illegible]

Aliens Order, 1920.

CERTIFICATE OF REGISTRATION

You must produce this certificate when required to do so by any Police Officer, Immigration Officer, or member of His Majesty's forces acting in the course of his duty.

Contents

From Bardo to Paradise

'Where are you from?' It's a simple enough question, right up there with 'what's your name?' or 'what do you do?' Whenever you get into conversation with someone new at a dinner party, these are the staple questions. I guess that knowing the answers helps people to frame an idea of who you are, your deeper identity.

Okay then. My name is Monica Devilliers. You may even have heard of me. I was the woman behind the fashion label Monica. I sold the business decades ago, but back in the 1960s it was a chic little fashion house where hip young things would shop for the latest trends. I was quite a big name in my day, but my route there was neither traditional nor easy.

Monica Devilliers. Or was that Monia Kowalska? Or Monique? In my lifetime, I have been known as all three. I still am, depending on who I'm talking to.

What about where I come from? There's no easy answer, and it's a question I always used to struggle with. 'How long have you got?' I usually want to reply. 'Do you mean now? Most recently? Where I grew up? Where I was born?' People close to me know that I grew up in a small mining village in the South Wales valleys. But that is just a tiny part of the story.

Back in the summer of 1966, when my doctor told me I was pregnant, the news knocked me for six. Not because I didn't want children; rather, the prospect of having a child forced me to think about my own childhood. I had hidden from the demons from that time of my life for many years.

I was born 21st January 1938, in the tiny little village of Les Baudrats, near the mining town of Montceau-les-Mines in Burgundy, central France. So I must be French then, right? Not really. We need to go back further, to before I was born even: back to a unique and turbulent moment in European history, and to an obscure village that found itself, unwittingly, caught up in it.

Today, it is difficult to fully appreciate the impacts of the First World War. France, for example, was officially on the winning side of the war, but when she tried to pick up as an industrial nation, she could not. There were simply not enough men left to work in all the factories, the steel works, and particularly the coal mines which fuelled them. Factory machinery lay quiet, blast furnaces cooled, trains and ships were left in their moorings, trains in their sheds. To say nothing of heating for homes, factories, offices and municipal buildings. Without coal, you could not function.

Meanwhile, on the other side of Europe, another nation with deep wounds to lick was Poland. Poland had a proud history as a nation in its own right, but for just over a century before the First World War, it had been non-existent, partitioned up between the Russians, the Prussians and the Austro-Hungarians. It is a period of Polish history known as 'The Partitioning' or 'The Annexation of Poland'. But throughout this century of subjection, the Polish people never lost their sense of identity. They maintained their language, their culture, their history and their traditions. Everyone had to learn two languages: Polish and German or Polish and Russian. They were always confident that, one day, they would somehow re-emerge as a proud and independent nation.

But for now, they had nowhere on a map to point to and call Poland. They were just like the Israelites of the Old Testament (an analogy that was not lost on them) – only, sadly, they were to have no Moses to lead them from captivity.

During the war, a lot of fighting had taken place in what was notionally Poland. Towns and cities had been razed to the ground and millions slaughtered. Unlike France, however, there was no pre-war normality that anyone could look forward to when it was all over. The country had been little more than a colony for over a century. During that period, it had fallen behind other nations, who had grown much more industrialised, and it was now a very poor relation to the rest of Europe. What little infrastructure that existed had been designed to serve its former masters. It was disjointed, outdated and not designed with the future of a new nation in mind.

Yet suddenly this *was* a new nation. As part of the post-war treaty with Germany, Poland was once more a nation in its own right. The second Polish Republic had been born. This was far from a steadying development for the Polish people, however. Over their long century of occupation, Poles had dreamed of independence, but when it came, it was not everything it was cracked up to be. Within a year of the First World War ending, Poland was already at war again, with both Czechoslovakia and Ukraine, in disagreements over sovereignty of territories and borders. The fledgling Polish government frequently collapsed or was dissolved, as different political factions fought for control. Meanwhile, the people in the provincial and rural backwaters starved.

One such backwater was a small historic town near the Czech border in the former Prussian-controlled partition of southwestern Poland, a crossing point on the Eastern Neisse river called Bardo. With a population of under a thousand, in any other part of Poland, Bardo would probably have been regarded as a village, and a small village at that. But all these things are relative, and in that part of the country, even such a speck on the ground as Bardo served as an administrative centre.

For the last 100 years, the governing Prussian authorities had called it by its German name, Wartha, but no one who lived in Bardo ever took after them. Bardo was a pretty little town, and its inhabitants were all very proud of it. It had a picturesque town square, edged with tall mediaeval town houses, and a historic bridge dating back to the fifteenth century. In its day, this bridge had put the town on the main trading route between Prague and Wroclaw, and from there to Warsaw and all the other cities of Poland. The town was also the seat of a historic monastery and basilica commemorating the miracle of the visitation of the Virgin Mary. In the Middle Ages, this had made it a destination for pilgrimage, and religion was still a very important part of life in Bardo.

If you head down a dirt track which starts on the riverbank opposite the southern edge of the town, after no more than a mile, in the shade of densely forested hills, you will find a small hamlet made up of three farms and a scattering of cottages. Those wooden cottages once housed the labourers who worked on those farms. It is in one of those cottages that my story begins. Both my grandmother and my mother were born there, and possibly many other descendants before them.

The interior of the cottage was very spartan, made up of one living room and one bedroom where the whole family slept. There was a woodburning iron stove in each room, but these were painfully inadequate against the cold that characterised much of the year. The air inside both rooms was always heavy with damp and chill. All the stoves seemed to do was make it smoky and smelly into the bargain. In the summer, though, the character of the cottage and the surrounding countryside changed dramatically. It was a very beautiful setting.

Leaving the coldness and harshness of winter to one side, it sounds peaceful, idyllic even. However, river crossing points on major routes near national borders have always been strategically important, and this is especially true in eastern Europe, where, for much of history, national borders have only ever been drawn in light pencil. As a result, over the centuries, Bardo was constantly getting sacked, invaded, burned to the ground, bombed or just basically flattened in whatever way was most fashionable at the time. The true miracle of Bardo was not so much the visitation of the Virgin, but simply the fact that it was still standing to commemorate the event.

*

My granny, whose name was Alinka, lived in a cottage with her own parents, Sophie and Josef, and her husband Zarec. They had two sons, Pawel and Michiek. My mother, Jasia, was not born until 1920. She was the archetypal war baby. During peacetime, the family could only be described as peasants, farm muscle living on the whim and benevolence of their landowners; during the war, they were cannon fodder.

Expectations were very different back then. It was considered a good year if everyone in the family survived the winter, or made it through whatever diseases or food shortages might at any given moment be sweeping through the town. It was a very meagre existence, right on the edge. During the First World War, Bardo was heavily shelled, and many buildings were in ruins. In our family, Zarec, Josef and Alinka's two brothers had all been conscripted into the German army and sent off to the Eastern Front to fight the Russians. The fighting had been ferocious, and the casualties sky high.

Things were not much easier back home. Alinka had to find ways of feeding the family, and that was getting harder and harder the longer the war went on. Any food that was available was diverted out to the troops on the front line. The livestock from the surrounding farms had gone virtually immediately after the war broke out. This meant that there was no money coming in either. Mind you, even if there had been, there would have been nothing to spend it on. The family had to survive on what they could grow themselves in very poor soil. In the spring and summer, that was just about feasible, but wintertime was cruel, and the winter of 1918 especially so. My uncles, Pawel and Michiek, became terribly malnourished. Already of a slight build, Michiek in particularly suffered badly. He was still skinny even when I knew him as an adult. These were years where growth and bone development were at a crucial stage, and that year of virtual starvation left Uncle Michiek with a limp for the rest of his life. Pawel was always a big lad, much more powerfully built and a few years older than his brother, so he had more resilience about him.

My great grandmother Sophie also became very ill, her resistance no doubt lowered by malnourishment, catching a fever in the late summer of 1918. She was bedridden, too weak to walk, and as the fever took its grip, she became unable to hold down food of any kind. She held on until the end of the war, no doubt hoping she would get to see her husband again, but that was not to be. Pretty much as soon as the armistice was signed in November, she passed away.

Near the end, Alinka, my grandmother, was sitting by the side of her bed. Alone in the room with her mother, all she could hear was the patient's breathing, irregular and unrhythmic. 'It's like I was sitting with her in a cellar with the door closed,' she remembered in later life. She could sense how every breath was becoming harder and harder to take. The sound of the breathing grew deeper, like her mother was moving further away, even though she remained lying in the bed next to her. Without her realising it, Alinka's breathing started to mimic her mother's, growing deeper, ragged, slowing... until it stopped completely. Alinka caught herself not breathing, and realised her mother just was not there anymore. She could see her, but her body was, somehow, visibly empty. Her soul had left its body, that was unmistakable.

For about twenty minutes, Alinka just sat there by the bed, still holding her mother's hand. She could feel nothing coming back. No grip, no feeling, just the weight of her bones. She cried for about an hour before leaving the room, then went straight to the priest.

Apparently his first question was how she was to pay for the funeral. The only things the family had of any value were a broach and some small bits of jewellery that had belonged to her now dead mother. She handed it all over to him and, would you believe it, was grateful he accepted it. Sadly, this began a regular pattern with my granny. In so many ways, she was the wisest and most intelligent woman I ever knew, but there was something about the Catholic Church that always blindsided her logic. The family were on the edge of starving to death, and the only objects of any value in the house, she gave to the damned priest. And what is worse, the priest accepted them, knowing full well that the family were starving, and that they had nothing to buy food with.

Alinka had the thankless task of writing to her father on the frontline to tell him the terrible news. Not knowing what impact it might have on him, she prayed every day at the basilica, as she had with her mother when she had been alive. Now her companions in prayer were the other women of the town; they all prayed that their families would be delivered from the horrors of war. But Alinka was never to see either of her brothers again. Both were killed in action in some meaningless skirmish, fighting for a cause they did not understand, for a country they neither belonged to nor cared anything about. Alinka only found out what had happened to her brothers when her father and her husband returned from the war. No one in the German authorities had felt they owed the family an explanation of how or where they had died, so no letter or telegram had ever been dispatched. What did two more dead Polish peasants matter to the Kaiser? Like I say: cannon fodder.

The morning Zarec and Josef returned from the war was misty and late in the year, the sun rising later in the day so that, while Alinka was drawing water from the well, the light was still quite low. She looked up momentarily and could make out two men in uniform walking down the track towards the hamlet. She dropped her bucket on the floor, letting the water spill as she ran up the track to meet them. She barely dared to hope. As she got closer, she could start to make out their faces through the mist, and she called to them excitedly.

'Papa! Zarec!'

Her father dropped the bag he was carrying from his shoulders and held out his arms to embrace her. '*Moj Koteczek*,' he said to her, as she ran into his arms. This means 'my little kitten', and it was the name he had called her since she had been a little baby. She had been a busy, curious child, interested in everything, and the name had stuck.

Zarec just trudged on, not even stopping to acknowledge her. She and her father chattered all the way back to the cottage, with Zarec a few paces ahead of them. At that point she had not asked about her brothers. For some reason she just assumed they would be joining them later on. She sang to herself while preparing a dinner for the family. There wasn't much, but there were enough vegetables and potato to make a soup, so that's what she did.

The bombshell about Alinka's two brothers didn't drop until the family were all seated at the table to eat dinner. 'Have you heard from either of them?' she asked excitedly. There was a protracted silence. Neither her father nor her husband could look her in the eye. Her face dropped and a tear formed. She could not help herself. Before either of them could say anything, she had run out of the cottage into the night air. She sat under a tree on the edge of the hamlet and buried her head between her knees to cry for their loss. She hadn't truly considered it possible that either of them would die. Maybe it had been their youthfulness or their optimism when they had left. For whatever reason, this news could not have been more of a surprise to her.

Alinka and the family had all hoped that, once the war was over, life would become more manageable. The men would come home from the front, the farm would once again have livestock that needed feeding and tending, there would be work, money coming in and food on the table. But living in Bardo, that was not to be. No sooner had Zarec and Josef returned from the First World War, having relinquished their call up to the German army, than they found themselves conscripted into the newly formed Polish Armed Forces, and were off fighting Czechoslovakia.

Alinka often commented that, looking back, she did not know how she ever coped with it. She had lost her mother and become aware of the loss of her two brothers in the space of a few months. She then had to watch as her father and husband returned from one war just to go straight back out to fight in another – and just as winter was taking a grip. She had to carry with her the very real fear that, if they did not return, she and her two boys might not survive. She knew how close to death they had already been, how fragile her grip on survival was. She also knew that, if Zarec did not return, their two children made a remarriage unlikely.

Things in Bardo were bad. And there seemed little hope in them getting better any time soon.

Poland and France had been allies for centuries. Some of Napoleon's most trusted generals had been Polish. So when a much reduced France threw her doors open to anyone who might wish to work in her mines, a specific agreement was made with Poland. Word of the warm reception received by Polish applicants spread amongst the troops fighting against the Czechs. Everyone had had a gut's full of war, poverty, death and starvation, to say nothing of a fragile Polish state that looked like it could collapse in on itself at any moment. The idea of leaving all this behind and heading to a new life in a civilised country, a country that would welcome you with open arms, was very appealing. What's more, the French were offering a modern home for every family, guaranteed work and decent wages.

What was there not to like? Before they had returned home from the fighting, Josef and Zarec had already decided: this was too good an opportunity to pass up. For the sake of Zarec and Alinka's boys, they owed themselves and the family a better life. As insignificant as they were in their capacity as peasants, they had proven themselves on the battlefield to be excellent soldiers. They had been promoted to corporal and sergeant respectively, and they had the respect of the men they fought with. As neither of them could read or write, they asked their platoon commander, the third son of a Polish count called Lieutenant Henrik Tomaszewski, if he could help them with their application, and naturally he agreed.

At last the fighting came to an end, as some faceless politicians no one had ever heard of made an agreement no one knew the details of. Josef and Zarec were discharged, and the two of them returned home to let Alinka know of the fait accompli: all being well, they were emigrating to France as a family. She said nothing, just took it in her stride. Inside, though, she was overjoyed. The cottage was filled with too many painful memories for her. She was at the stage where she believed that anything would be better than this.

Within a few weeks, Tomaszewski, who lived in a grand house only a few miles outside Bardo, arrived at the family cottage on a beautiful white gelding, to read the reply that had come to him from France. The whole family came from the cottage to meet him. Alinka even curtsied as he got off his horse, having never met a noble man before. For him to have ridden out personally was a lovely gesture and more than anyone had expected him to do. He was very proud to announce to them that their application had been approved and that they would soon be bound for France. The vodka was duly opened, and the three men sat around the family dinner table and drank to celebrate the good news.

Alinka desperately searched for some bread to have while they drank, but there was none in the house. She darted next door to borrow some from her neighbours.

'Whose is that horse?' they asked curiously, as they handed over what little bread they had.

'It belongs to Count Tomaszewski's son,' she beamed proudly. 'He is a friend of Zarec and my father from the army, and he has come to visit and give us some wonderful news. We are going to France!'

Her neighbours stared back in total amazement. This information was too spectacular to take in. Alinka skipped back to the house with pride, knowing that, in a matter of days, the whole town would have heard the news. At the end of the day, as Tomaszewski staggered out of the cottage, all the neighbours had come out to see him for themselves. Even if he was not at his best, a noble man in their corner of the woods was something to see. A few of them helped Zarec and Josef bundle him onto his horse, and off he trotted – possibly relying more on his horse's homing instincts than his own abilities.

*

For modern sensibilities, it might seem a bit odd that the fate of the family should be decided between my grandfather and his father-in-law, without any consultation with my granny. But that is how things were done back then, and this was not the first time the terms of her life had been dictated to her. Her marriage to Zarec had been decided in pretty much the same way. He was far from her natural choice of husband. He may have made a good soldier – good with a rifle, good with his fists – but in pretty much every other respect the man was a total idiot. And a violent one at that. As I mentioned earlier, my granny was a fiercely intelligent woman, and in different circumstances, I believe she could have been very accomplished, either in business or medicine or as an academic. But such a prospect was totally unobtainable back then to a woman born to her station in society.

Sadly for her, her future had been mapped out when she was just a teenaged girl, when she had a fling with a boy and got pregnant. Devout Catholics in a small town where everyone knew everybody's business, the family were deeply shamed. She was beaten by her father and prohibited from leaving the cottage. Her parents and the parish priest were awful to her and did everything they could to drag from her the name of the father, but she refused to give him up. I'm not sure he deserved her silence or would have been quite so loyal to her if the tables had been turned. Whoever he was, he never put his hand up to it.

Eventually the only solution that was acceptable to the family and the priest was to marry her off to a boy in the town who otherwise would have been unmarriable – basically, the village idiot. And that was my grandfather. He understood nothing of what went on in the world or even around him. He went through life with a big chip on his shoulder and settled every dispute, no matter how minor, with aggression or violence. She never said it out loud, but I am sure my granny would have secretly traded his life for that of one of her brothers, but it was not to be.

I think this episode was the source of much of the guilt my granny carried around with her for the rest of her life – a sense of guilt which made her forever beholden to the Church. I think she thought that her many trials were God's punishment for her succumbing to temptation and having sex. She was forever a slave to that guilt, even if the fruit of it was Pawel. No one could have known then what a hero he would turn out to be.

Shortly before the family were due to set off for France, my mother, Jasia, was born. She would be the last member of the family to be born on Polish soil, although this was a milestone they could only appreciate in hindsight.

Now my granny Alinka, her husband Zarec, her father Josef, her two sons Pawel and Michiek, and a tiny little baby girl, Jasia, were about to set off to start a new life away from everything and everyone they had ever known. The family packed ready for the journey ahead of them. Josef had made a wooden suitcase which measured about a meter wide by sixty centimetres down and about forty deep. The family of six packed everything they owned into it. I've still got it. I store books in it and keep it under a window seat in my study at home. It is a great leveller. Sometimes when I think that my life is shit or that the world is against me, I just look at it, remember what it signifies, and get over myself. Everything the family owned used to fit in that suitcase. Things really are not so bad, are they?

One of the family's old neighbours, Tadek Mishak, got permission from the farmer to hook the farm horse up to the cart they used for transporting hay out to the herd in the furthest fields. All the neighbours came out to wave them off. My granny, my uncles and my mother were put in the back of the cart with the suitcase. It was a drizzly day and the cart was completely open, so they all huddled under a blanket to try and keep warm and dry. Josef and Zarec rode up front with Tadek, and they drove out to the railway station, where they would catch the first of many trains to take them more than a thousand miles over five days to their new home.

Their journey took them across Poland, Germany, Belgium and France. It was already a few years since the end of the First World War, but still so much of the continent lay in ruins. Sometimes they would travel for mile after mile and see nothing but rubble; occasionally one building might be intact, maybe a single church spire emerging from the ruins to commemorate that once this had been a town where families lived, worked, made plans, married and had children.

The Poles who took the French up on their invitation did not have any say on where they would end up, not that it would have made any difference if they had. My granny had never travelled more than ten miles outside of Bardo, and while my grandfather and great grandfather had travelled extensively in the war, they had only ever gone where their commanders had taken them. As it turns out, after the Russian Revolution had closed the Eastern Front, they had found themselves transferred west, and had actually fought in trenches on French soil. However, they had had no idea where they were; they could not have told the difference between Köln or Calais.

The majority of the Poles who emigrated to France in this period ended up in the industrialised northern regions of the country, around cities like Lille and Bethune, where a vast coal field had the greatest need for bodies. Certainly that's where most of my grandfather's regiment ended up. But it was not to be the destination for my family, something I am very grateful for. Not that I have an issue with Lille. It is a wonderful city. But the industrial landscape around it, especially between the wars, was a dark satanic one, filled with factory chimneys belching black smoke into smog-filled skies, a long, flat, boring vista, only broken up by slag heaps and pit head winches. I think the shock to a family who had lived their lives surrounded by lush greenery and rural tranquillity would have been overwhelming. Thankfully, their destination could not have been more different.

If we were playing a word association game and I was to say to you, 'Burgundy,' what do you think you might you come back with? 'Wine' is usually the first thing. And there is no doubt that Burgundy produces some of the greatest wines in the world. Maybe gastronomy? Escargots? History? Culture? Sophistication? Maybe Charolais beef?

Bresse chicken? Morvan-cured pork, sausages and ham? All would be bang on the money. For much of history, the dukes of Burgundy were more powerful than the kings of France. And they built beautiful cities like Dijon, Autun, Macon and Beaune, amazingly opulent châteaux like at Couche and Ancy le Franc, vineyards that are the envy of the wine-producing world, and fostered a rich culture and heritage to boot.

One word you probably would not come up with, however, is 'coal'. But slap bang in the middle of all this high living and sophistication is a tiny coal field which is relatively unknown outside the region itself. It centres around the towns of Montceau-les-Mines and Le Creusot, near Chalon-sur-Saone, and is linked to the rest of France by the Canal du Centre and the other waterways of the river Saone. Compared to the coal fields around Lille, it was like another planet. While the coal mine itself looked much the same as any other, you only had to walk a mile or so in any direction to find yourself in beautiful rolling countryside. And all those amazing places, like Beaune, Autun, Couche and Macon, were only a little further afield again.

Of course, when finally the family arrived, this was the last thing on their minds. They reported to the administrator at the Hotel de Ville at Montceau-les-Mines, not one of them able to speak a word of French. But this was an eventuality the French authorities were more than prepared for, and interpreters were on hand. The authorities had thought of everything, and the process for patriating these Poles into France was beautifully efficient, kicking into action like a well-oiled machine.

The family were taken from the centre of Montceau-les-Mines, in the shadow of the mines there, and onto Saunvigne, where the men were to work. They passed along the banks of the canal and out into the tranquil countryside to the little village of Les Baudrat. On arrival they were met by a Polish member of the village council, who showed them to their new home. It was a typical turn-of-the-century French worker's cottage: a single storey building with a high-pitched red-tiled roof. The outer walls were rendered the colour of sand and there was exposed brickwork around the tall sash windows, each one flanked on either side by full length, brick-red wooden shutters. Each house was divided into two, with one family living at the front and another family at the back, both having access to a cellar. The whole building was moated by a huge garden which was split into allotments, so each family had their own space to grow food. There was a well in the garden and fruit trees dotted along the back fence. Theirs was one of about 500 in the village, all of them identical and all based along the same handful of interconnected, tree-lined streets.

As soon as she saw it, my granny just fell to her knees and wept. Her two sons, exhausted from the journey, fell to their knees too, wrapped their arms around her neck and wept with her. And there they stayed, rooted to the spot in the middle of the road. She once told me that the house was the most beautiful thing she had ever seen in her life and that she could not believe that this was going to be their new home.

Before the Poles arrived, Les Baudrat had been just a couple of cottages and a derelict mill, nestled by a small, wood-lined lake. In that regard, it had not been that different from the hamlet my family had lived in near Bardo. The lake was fed by some small, fast flowing streams. There was marshland on one side, woods on another, and clear open countryside all around. The mine at Saunvigne was hidden from sight by the woods and other houses, although it was close enough for you to hear the siren calling the changing of the shifts.

The French had built the community up to accommodate the newcomers, and to the Poles, the wide, tree-lined, cobbled streets resembled the smartest districts of Wroclaw. The tall stone cottages were palatial compared to the squat, damp wooden ones they had left behind. And the beautiful, peaceful countryside around them was not that different from home. Plus, there was good fishing on the lake.

In addition to now having a predominantly Polish population, Les Baudrat and other villages like it had a Polish village council representative, a church with a Polish priest who heard confession in Polish and where they sang Polish hymns, and a school with Polish-speaking teachers. The butcher and the baker were both Polish, and while there was no candlestick maker, if there ***had*** been, he would have been Polish too. There were no hindrances to anything, even for a family unable to speak a word of French. When the men showed up to work in the mine, their entire shift was made up of Polish workers. The only Frenchman among them was the foreman. And he'd learned to speak Polish!

In the house there were three rooms. Alinka, Zarec and the three children shared one room; Josef, my great grandfather, had a room to himself; and the third room was a kitchen-cum-dining and living room.

Pawel was by now sixteen years old, old enough to get a job at the mine with his father and grandfather. They put him to work in the stables, looking after one of the pit ponies, which earned him the nickname 'Slange', the name of the horse he kept. My grandfather and great grandfather went to work on the coalface. For the first time in his life, Michiek had some schooling, an experience he was not as grateful for as you might have thought! And Alinka was at home, bringing up little Jasia, tending to the garden, preparing meals and keeping house. She also took it upon herself to learn French, probably the first person in the village who bothered. As I said, she was a very intelligent woman. She would also go to Mass every day, and twice on Sundays, and would drag the children along with her. Now that Pawel spent his days in the company of working men much older and more mature than him, he was learning to stretch his wings a bit, and would frequently try and resist. But he would still be young enough for a clip around the ear for a few years yet, to put a stop to all that nonsense.

I often wondered what direction Alinka's life would have taken had she not got pregnant so young. She definitely would not have wound up marrying Zarek. I do believe that she had the calling of a nun though. Her devotion to the Church and her intelligence would have made her a real asset to any teaching convent. As much as I would never wish myself out of existence, I often felt sorry for her that she never got to realise her ambition. It would have suited her down to the ground. As it was, the Church's loss was my gain. My granny was always the member of my family I felt closest to growing up – far closer than I ever felt to my own mother.

Within a year of arrival, Les Baudrat's status as the family's new home was confirmed when Alinka got pregnant again, giving birth to another little girl: little Mira, a sister and companion for my mother, and the first of the family to be born on French soil, another milestone.

In the years that followed, my family's lives, though simple by modern standards, were idyllic. The memory of what they had endured during the years before remained, but as the family turned towards a brighter future, the shadows fell behind them.

Meet the Family

As tough as working underground was in those days, Josef and Zarec took to it like ducks to water.

Josef, my great grandfather, was quite a simple, stoic man. He was very tall, well over six foot, powerfully built and a man of few words. He communicated predominantly through pointing, gesturing and making approving or disapproving grunts, and these were not always that easy to tell apart. All his life he had toiled on the land, where good conversation was not an asset. Getting your head down, doing a solid day's work and being dependable and reliable was what farmers looked for from their labourers, and that pretty much summed up what he gave them.

After that, he had been a soldier on the front line, where expectations were much the same. Now he worked underground. And coal miners, as you can no doubt guess, needed some of the same stuff as well. However, much more conversation was expected from a miner, much more male bonding and banter between co-workers. Everyone had nicknames, and his was 'Grabarz', which means gravedigger. This was not meant to sound like an American wrestler; it was more to do with his rather dour, silent demeanour. At first his co-workers thought Josef was struggling with the move to France, that he was home sick or that the work disagreed with him. But as time passed, they realised that this was just how he was.

The social side to working in the mines went further than comradeship underground. The union also organised dinners and dances and day trips. This was all a bit alien to Josef, but he always went along, signing up for everything. He had a very strong belief in toeing the line, a keen sense of what was expected of him. But as for joining in, I don't think he ever even cracked a smile. There are countless photographs of him taken at various events down the years, from union dinners to family weddings, right up until he was quite an old man, and in every single one he is standing in the background with a dolorous facial expression and a glass of vodka in his hand. In these same photographs, everyone else will be having a great time, smiling, laughing, raising their glasses or dancing. But there he stands, disconnected from the scene, looking almost like he isn't really there. Like the camera has somehow caught the image of a passing ghost. I often wonder what it would have taken for him to have had some fun. Not that he was an unpleasant man or a mean man. He was actually quite generous. But he was what we would describe today as a mood hoover.

He worked hard though. He always put in a good shift at the pit. And he was a good union man, never missing a meeting. If there was work that needed doing, putting up posters or handing out leaflets to potential new recruits, all they had to do was ask him and they knew it would be done. As time went by, this meant that he earned the trust and respect of both his supervisors and foremen and of his union committee. So they made him an official. If ever there were important negotiations to be made with the pit bosses, he was always present in the room. What possible purpose that could have served, I have no idea. I doubt very much that he ever contributed to the meetings, and as he was illiterate, he could not even have taken notes. But I think he would have got a lot out of it, a chance to fulfil his unshakable sense of duty, which was as close to fun as he could have.

When I was a little girl, Josef used to bounce me on his knee. When English-speaking parents bounce children on their knees, they might sing 'Half a Pound of Tupenny Rice'. In my childhood we had a Polish nursery song which went:

Jedzie, jedzie pan, pan,
na koniku sam, sam,
a za Panem chłop, chłop,
hop, hop, hop, hop, hop, hop,
a za chłopem żydóweczka,
co skakała jak małpeczka
hyc, hyc, hyc.

And so on.

It's just a nonsense song, the knee-bouncing starting off slowly, the song going, '*this is how the lady rides,*' then accelerating as the singing continues, '*and this is how the gentleman rides.*' Finally, the knees really get bouncing as we get to the third bit: '*this is the way the farm hand rides*'. I used to laugh like a drain at this, insisting on starting it over again and again. And bless him, every time he would oblige. He even managed to break a smile while he was doing so. Not a big beaming one, but there was no doubt that his lips were curling up at the edges. I always thought he drew particular pride from the last verse of this song. Having spent so many years of his life as a farmhand, perhaps he felt like he was singing about himself.

It was a shame he was so silent most of the time, as he had a lovely voice and really could hold a note. He had a deep, resonating bass baritone, and I am sure if he had ended up in Wales rather than France, like I did in later life, he would have found his place in a colliery male voice choir. It is a peculiarity of both the Poles and the Welsh that, when they are celebrating, everyone sings really miserable songs. In Wales nothing goes down better at a wedding than all the guests singing 'Myfanwy' at the end of the evening. In Poland it's 'Goralu, czy ci nie zal'. Both have exactly the same effect. All the old ladies burst into tears and everyone goes home happy.

I only knew Josef as a little girl, and in a house as busy and frantic as ours, someone who didn't say much was easy not to notice. He died when I was quite young. Maybe I was five or six. He was ninety-four years old when he died. That's a good innings even now, but for a coal miner in the early twentieth century it was unheard of. He even got a write up in the local newspaper. My granny told them that he was a loving father, grandfather and great grandfather, a hard-working man who was a good provider for the family and always went to Mass; his old union buddies, meanwhile, made him sound like a hero of socialism and a soldier of the revolution. From what I knew about him, I really think that was unlikely. But who knows? Maybe he had a secret side which he never brought home. The whole thing gave the family our fifteen minutes of fame, and even French families we didn't know stopped my granny in the street to give her their condolences.

When her father died, my granny was totally devastated. He was the last of the family she had grown up with. Her brothers had gone, her mother had gone, now her father had gone too. She was the last one left. And even though he had treated her terribly over her pregnancy out of wedlock, and even though she blamed him for forcing her into her less-than-happy marriage, she still had always loved him.

When it came to organising his funeral, she had to fuss about every detail. Everything had to be just right. That meant, of course, that after the funeral there would be a wake back at the house. His colleagues, people she hardly knew, would be there, both French and Polish, and they would be bringing their wives. It was very important to her that she gave a good impression. The whole house was scrubbed and cleaned from top to bottom. Best linen had to be bought for the occasion and laid on the table, and for some reason she became obsessed with the idea that there should be a good photograph of her father, on display for all to pay their respects.

This presented a problem. Today, people are always taking photographs. It does not even need to be a special occasion. For most of Josef's lifetime, however, having a photograph taken was a big deal. And expensive too. Certainly no one in the family had ever owned a camera. And as I said, throughout his life, he had spent every social event in the background. Even though he was present in thousands of photographs, it was always a group shot, with him in the background or the back row, partially obscured by the person in front of him. There was only one single photograph she could find which did him justice. It had been taken when he was discharged from the army after the war. He had been a young man back then, with dark hair, quite handsome in a rugged, lived in sort of a way, and, in this photograph at least, properly groomed and smartly dressed. And most importantly, he was in the photograph on his own. It was exactly what she was looking for. He could even pass off as looking nearly happy in it.

She found a suitable frame, dusted it down and positioned it with pride in the centre of the kitchen table. Now every detail was perfect. Or was it? As smart as my great grandfather looked in this photograph, there was one tiny flaw: he was quite clearly wearing a German military uniform from the First World War. Complete with Iron Cross, no less! To say that it got a mixed reception at the wake would be more than an understatement. Some of the French guests had to reach for their reading glasses; they really could not believe what they were seeing! Even the priest, Polish by birth but whose family had fought on the Russian side, nearly spat his drink out when he saw it. My granny, oblivious to this faux pas, stood by, proudly and graciously smiling, taking the plaudits from the other wives as to the beautiful flowers in her garden and the moistness of her cakes. Nobody said anything to my granny about the photograph. Everyone was just too polite.

Now that Josef was gone, there was now no one around to keep Zarec in check. He had a ferocious temper and frequently went too far. I think I have already made it clear that I had zero respect for my grandfather. He was a persistent bully, a wife beater and a child beater. When Josef got old and close to retirement, Zarec assumed the duty of head of the household. No one told him he needed to. It was just a thought that lodged itself in his tiny brain. It was also a role he was completely inadequate at performing. He thought that the head of the household should be sullen and unapproachable at all times, and that the job of an alpha male was to criticise or ridicule his wife and children.

You always knew when it was coming. There would be days that he would come home from work spoiling for a fight before he had even walked through the door. When he walked into the kitchen, everyone would avoid eye contact and busy themselves with whatever they were doing. Maybe my mum and my granny would be cooking dinner together, maybe Mira would be peeling some potatoes, while Michiek read a manual about a machine at work and Pawel repaired his work overalls. But someone was going to get it. You just never knew who.

He would start with a criticism; whatever you were doing, either you shouldn't be doing it, or you were doing it wrong. Then you'd be mocked or ridiculed until he could goad a look, a tut or a sigh or a roll of the eyes. And then off would come the belt, and he would beat the living daylights out of you.

Growing up in an environment like that, you can go one of two ways. You either observe that behaviour and vow never to repeat it, or you take it as an example to emulate. My aunty and uncles all went down the route of swearing they would never behave like that with their own children. But not my mother. She looked on it as a bloody training course.

When Josef had been alive, he had always been able to stop Zarec in his tracks. He did not need to get physically involved; a disapproving 'cut that out' yelled from any corner of the house with that deep booming voice of his was enough to bring things to a close. In the end, Pawel stepped up, thank God. He was a grown man by this point, already old and strong enough to stop his adopted father physically, even if vocally he did not have the gravitas of his grandfather. After a furious rant when Zarec started on my mother, then switched his attentions to my granny because she tried to defend her daughter, something snapped in Pawel. He stood between his father and his mother and held his father back from kicking her on the ground. He did not use any violence himself, only restraint, but because by now Pawel was such a big bear of a man, a good foot taller than his father, with hands the size of buckets, there was nothing Zarec could do. As stupid as Zarec was, even he had managed to work out for himself that, if Pawel ever actually did punch him on the nose, then he would not be getting back up again anytime soon.

This incident didn't stop Zarec from being abusive, but from that moment on, there was at least a way of making him stop for the rest of the evening. And that had to be good enough. Reluctantly, Pawel became the family-fight umpire.

Living with abuse is a horrific thing, and everyone needs to find their own way of dealing with it, otherwise it becomes all too easy to be ground down. My granny would take solace from keeping busy. She had our household to manage: all the cleaning, gardening, food preparation and cooking. She also had her young daughters to bring up. Then she would tend to the grave of her father, and bury herself in her favourite distraction of all: going to church. If there had been a Mass every hour of every day, I am sure that she would have gone to them all. Through all the shit life threw at her, her faith remained unshakable. Either that, or it at least gave her a place of peace where she could hide herself. Whichever, in later life I envied her that.

I used to go with her as often as I could. I loved my granny. When I was growing up, she seemed to be the only island of sanity in my mad family. Most of my happiest memories as a little girl involved handing my granny wildflowers, for her to arrange on my great grandfather's grave, before going together to church to pray silently, clutching our rosaries in the hour before Mass. And after Mass, heading home to make dinner. She was a true matriarch, one of those Amazonian women who cannot stay still for even a second. She was incapable of just sitting down – even if we were in someone else's house! Throughout dinner she would constantly be getting up to wash something or prepare something else. Watching her in a kitchen was like watching gnats dancing round a streetlamp, full of furious motion, urgency in every move.

She adored all of her children and grandchildren. She was the ying to Zarec's yang in that respect. Nothing was too much trouble. If Jasia wanted help with some needlework while her mother was serving up dinner, then dinner could wait, she'd be there. Or if Mira had learned a new song in school and wanted her mum to listen to it, everything would be put on hold until she had sung her last note.

Every generation has its own subtle distinctions from the one that went before it. Kids rarely grow up with an unchanged set of values to those of their parents. But by any measure, the divide between my grandparent's generation and that of my parents was a chasm.

Zarec and Alinka had been born in another century, in another country, as peasants living on the land. Growing up, their guiding forces had been their parents and the Church, and really nothing else. But Pawel, Michiek, Mira and my mother grew up amidst a totally different set of influences. Even though Polish was the language spoken in the home, Poles their own age spoke French to each other. Jasia and Mira both had the opportunity to go to school, to learn to read and write, something neither of their parents had done. And working amongst thousands of other workers, rather than a handful of labourers on a farm, with a cinema and theatre a short walk away, opened their eyes to things their parents had never even considered.

Nothing brought home the scale of the changes the family had seen more vividly than when, in later life, Pawel glibly commented over dinner that he had been born before the Wright brothers had first achieved flight, and had lived to see a man land on the moon.

The family now lived and worked in an industrialised conurbation. Yes, Les Baudrat was a village, but the nearby Montceau-les-Mines was a decent-sized town, and they soon had friends there. This introduced them to new political influences, like socialism and communism, concepts which had terrified Josef's generation. It also meant they had access to new cultural influences, music like jazz, for example. All their parents had known were regional folk songs. This was the dawning of a new world.

Pawel was the closest thing to a bridge between the generations. The eldest child in the family, he had been born in Poland and was a boy of sixteen when he had moved to France. He was able to see the whole chapter of the family's migration from start to finish. He understood how different their lives were now compared to how they had been before. Despite his huge stature and strength, Pawel was the stereotypical gentle giant. He had inherited his mother's sensitivity and his grandfather's height. He looked out for his younger brother, Michiek, who after a short education followed the rest of the men in the family down the pit. Pawel showed him the ropes, introduced him around and made sure he fitted in. Michiek was a fraction of the size of his brother. He was spindly and thin, not really suited to manual work on the coal face, especially given his slightly deformed foot. Luckily, his brother and grandfather's influence got him a chance to train up as a mine electrician, a move that not only suited him well, but set him up for life.

Pawel was just as important a figure in the life of his sisters, perhaps even more so, as they were the babies of the family. He always made sure they were looked after. In that respect, he acted like the father his own father had failed so dismally to be.

His role as surrogate father was further cemented when he took a wife, the ever-effervescent Nadia. She was another tour de force. They say men look for a wife who is like their mother, and my God, Nadia was like Alinka on acid. She was a tiny little thing; standing next to Pawel she just about came up to his chest, like a little Oompa-Loompa. But what she lacked in stature, she made up for in energy, resourcefulness and drive. She certainly squared Pawel up, and was a huge help to Alinka in running the house and family life, especially when she got older.

The couple were not in a position to get a house of their own, so they lived with the rest of the family in the little three-roomed house in Les Baudrat. Zarec, Alinka and Michiek had one room, Pawel, Nadia and the girls had the other, the girls at this point being teenagers. It was cramped and far from ideal, but they managed. The marriage had a strange effect on Zarec, who, just as quickly as he had assumed the role of head of the household, now relinquished it to Pawel. His new role was something akin to that of 'deeply unpleasant lodger who can't be evicted'.

Then There Was Me

When my mother was fifteen years old, in 1935, she was sharing a bedroom with her younger sister, her eldest brother and his wife. She had been attending school in the village, and she was blossoming into a very attractive young woman – not the brightest, but very pretty, an asset that had not gone unnoticed by the young men of Les Baudrat.

Around this time, Pawel was quite involved in the Communist Party in Montceau-les-Mines. His grandfather, Josef, still alive at the time, had been a union man since he'd started in the pit, but only because his co-workers had told him it was the right thing to do. Zarec understood even less than Josef and had nothing to do with the movement. Pawel initially joined because his grandfather had, but when Josef started to get promoted in the union ranks, Pawel took more of an interest. He took advantage of the fact that the union offered schooling to illiterate members, and through these he learned to read and write. Like a lot of men working in industrialised parts of Europe between the wars, he began to read up on what socialism and communism was all about, and he became a disciple of communism. He joined the Communist Party, attended meetings and made friends amongst the ranks of the membership.

One of the people he acquainted himself with was a showoff and self-professed firebrand called Stefan Kowalski, who would ultimately become my father. Stefan would have slotted right into 1960s Chelsea; he spent a lot of his life pretending to be more than he really was. He was a regular at the Communist Party meetings, where he would frequently get on his soapbox and wave his fist in the air, professing that 'workers needed to throw down their tools and seize the state, for a better future for our children' and other such clichés and catchphrases he'd heard elsewhere. He would only be able to declare such things in Polish, however, as he never learned a word of French. He relied totally on Pawel to be his interpreter. Everyone at those meetings was very impressed with him. The usual subjects for discussion were a tad more pedestrian. Meetings were typically filled by members' moaning about the inadequacies of the local union officials, who were too old, not radical enough, or all in the pockets of the bosses, depending on who you listened to. Talk about seizing the state was very exotic by comparison.

Stefan had had a very different upbringing from my mother's family. His family had only arrived in France comparatively recently, and the part of Poland they had moved from could not have been more different from Bardo. Stefan and his younger sister, Anetka, were from Gdansk, a huge industrial city with a commercial and a military port on the Baltic Sea. After Warsaw, it was the biggest city in Poland and a far cry from the tiny hamlet of wooden cottages my grandparents had left behind.

Because they were from a big city, Stefan and his family rather looked down their noses at the country bumpkins they now found themselves surrounded with. Stefan never stopped complaining about how boring Montceau was compared to Gdansk. But despite this and the difference in their ages, Stefan and Pawel got on like a house on fire. I think Pawel was seduced by Stefan's big city swagger and self-confidence, which bordered on arrogance. Neither of these were common attributes among the other people he knew. The two of them would frequently meet to discuss politics over a bottle of vodka. They would talk about their ambitions for a fairer society, run by the workers for the workers, talking about plots like two little boys comparing toys.

Stefan was also a musician, playing the accordion, the banjo and the harmonica, self-taught in all. It made him a good person to know if you wanted to get invited to parties. There would inevitably be a singsong at the end of the night, and Stefan was usually called upon to provide the accompaniment. He knew all the best Polish folk songs to make everybody cry.

My mother was also very impressed by Stefan's bravado. She ran into him one day when he came to the house to meet Pawel. She flirted with him – very obviously, it seemed to her – but he was a bit too full of himself to notice. However, Pawel was more attentive, and from then on he tried not to bring Stefan to the house if he could help it. But though Stefan lived in a different village, it was still part of 'Little Poland', and that year there were at least two weddings where he and my mother could meet, plus the dances held on 1st May (Workers Day) and 11th November (Polish national day), where all the Poles would dress their children up in national costume, parade through the town and in the evening have a big shindig. And so their courtship began.

While my mother was pretty, her conversation wasn't up to much. I am fairly sure Stefan was flattered by her attention but had no intentions at all of marrying her. However, as so often happens, he inadvertently got her pregnant. He must have tried every trick in the book to wriggle out of his responsibility, but Josef, Zarec and Pawel made quite a persuasive case, no doubt spelling out that the alternative was to be thrown into the Canal du Centre with stones tied to his feet. So one night he went home with them and proposed.

My mother, of course, was utterly oblivious to the fact that this was a proposal under duress. She thought it was all a fairytale. She could not quite believe it when both the timetable and the guest list for the wedding were kept so short, immediate family only. She wanted everyone there. She spent the whole of her wedding day in a big sulk; this was decidedly not how she had imagined her wedding day.

After the wedding, the happy couple moved in with Stefan's family. Stefan's mother had hoped her son would do better for himself than the daughter of some mad peasant who could barely string a sentence together, and this was a sentiment she was happy to make clear. Stefan's sister, Anetka, didn't like my mother either. Partly she saw her new sister-in-law's prettiness as a threat, but also she thought her a bit of a yokel. Anetka was not exactly a dazzling intellect herself, but she always considered herself superior to my mother.

And so began an era of married bliss, an era that, if it existed at all, was decidedly short-lived. Within a few months Stefan got thrown a lifeline. The Spanish Civil War had broken out, and by 1937 the Republican Alliance was crying out for volunteers to swell their ranks and suppress the revolt. Stefan could not believe his luck. He had long pretended at being a budding revolutionary, a soldier of the people and the workers. It was his duty to keep the red flag flying. So he volunteered – he volunteered so fast his feet barely touched the ground. He'd always hated Montceau-les-Mines, and now he was stuck there with a pregnant woman he had been trapped into marrying, enduring the disapproving and disappointed looks of his family day in, day out. Being shot at by fascists seemed to him a much better gig.

When he announced his intentions, full of all the drama and vitriol you would expect, my mother wept. Pawel, by way of contrast, was moved by the sentiments of international solidarity expressed by his friend, and he volunteered too. As we have already mentioned, Pawel was quite used to getting some abuse at home from his father; however, the roasting he got that night from Nadia was more than anything Franco's forces could have mustered. She absolutely wiped the floor with him. The days of the man of the house making life-changing decisions without involving his wife were over.

In her own way Alinka was also angry with her son, though she was unable to express it; no one got a word in edgeways that evening, around Nadia's rant. Alinka's reservations were not only that Pawel was putting himself in danger; the Catholic Church was very supportive of Franco's revolt. In Mass on Sundays the priest would frequently ask the congregation to pray for the rebels fighting the good fight in Spain. He would describe their struggle in the same terms as a crusade.

Pawel's decision put her at unexpected odds with the Church. But, resourceful woman that she was, she was able to reconcile it by praying that Pawel and Stefan would come home safely from their own battles, but that Franco would win the conflict over all.

Stefan and Pawel's volunteering gave the local branch of the Communist Party an idea. To drum up more support for the Spanish socialists and to showcase themselves as a party of action, they borrowed an open-sided truck, draped a red flag on one side and a Spanish flag on the other, and arranged to drive Stefan, Pawel and the other handful of local volunteers through the town centre and all the mining villages round and about. The idea was to parade the men as heroes, and for them to receive the rapturous, admiring applause of the town folk as they passed by. Stefan loved that idea. If there was one thing that man adored it was being adored, and he made sure he had a place right at the front of the truck, where everyone could see him. Off the truck rumbled, the men on the back smiling and waving at passers-by, looking forward to receiving the recognition of the community.

The reality of this parade, however, was nothing so glamorous as they had anticipated. All they generated was a lot of quizzical stares, and questions as to why they had seen fit to assemble on the back of a truck just to tool around waving at people.

Within a week, the revolutionaries were packed onto a train and off they went. My father hammed it up like he had already been martyred, clutching his heart and blowing kisses to everyone on the platform. My mother wailed uncontrollably, while everyone else rolled their eyes and tutted at her. As soon as the train was out of sight, she hastily moved back in with her parents. It had been pretty awful living with Stefan's family even when he was there, but being there on her own was going to be unbearable. Also, she was by now heavily pregnant. She wanted to be comfortable, surrounded by people she could rely on to fuss over her. Her homecoming meant another reshuffle of rooms. Mira, my mother and Nadia were in one room, with Michiek now sharing a room with his parents and his grandfather. He was twenty-seven at the time.

*

When they arrived in Spain, Pawel and Stefan were deployed into the International Brigade, which over the course of two years would see 60,000 foreign volunteers join up to fight for the Spanish government alongside its own forces and supporting militia groups. In the early stages, both men stayed in touch with the family with weekly letters, but these grew less frequent as the fighting became more regular and intense.

Stefan and Pawel remained together in Spain, serving in the same places, doing the same things, with the same people, sharing the same experiences, but you would never know it from their letters. Pawel had always been a matter-of-fact sort of a person, and his dry missives back to his loved ones read something like:

> *This week we have been mostly training. The Nationalist army are trying to cut Catalunya off from the rest of Spain so I think when we finish here on Friday we will be moved out to Barcelona where a lot of fighting is taking place right now.*
>
> *It's been lovely and warm the past couple of days and there's a guy here from Lille whose family come from Pilce. What a small world!*

As Pawel had learned to write in France, his letters were always written in French, rather than Polish, which meant that Stefan had no idea what he was writing, even if he was looking over his shoulder at the time. What my father would have made of his compatriot's style, we will never know. His own account of the same week read:

> *Since Monday I have been crawling on my belly with my dagger between my teeth. The Nationalist and Nazi devilish forces are everywhere, and I must defeat them at all costs. Every time I see a mother running for cover with her child, I think of my Jasia, and it reminds me how I must liberate these people from the tyranny they face.*

Do not weep for me if I should die here. But take solace from the bravery of those around me like Pawel who must fight on.

There is a chance that this early account was part of a plan. If Stefan could plant the seed that he might be killed in action, no one would be surprised if he never went back to Montceau again. It could be the perfect cover. This really is not something I would put past him, at least at the start of his campaign. However, his experience of the war would sober and change my father forever.

The Spanish Civil War was already in full swing when the two men got to Spain. Back in February 1936, a socialist alliance party called the Popular Front had won the majority of seats in the national government, but despite this they were unpopular with large swathes of the population. Those who had previously been the ruling classes – wealthy industrialists, Catholic bishops and cardinals, senior military personnel, as well as monarchists – rejected the socialist government. The early months of their administration were plagued by over 300 large scale and paralysing strikes. A general culture of lawlessness spread throughout the country, with churches and the offices of newspapers set on fire. Cries came from multiple quarters to depose the government. In July 1936, an extreme right-wing fanatic called José Calvo Sotelo was assassinated by government security forces and that lit the fuse. Within three weeks a general in the Spanish army, General Goded, led his forces in a coup in Barcelona. Simultaneously, other generals, including Franco, staged similar uprisings in all Spain's other major cities. This was a swift, decisive action intended to overthrow the Republican government and impose a right-wing, monarchist and fascist alternative – but as quite often happens in wars, things did not pan out as expected. The uprising was successful in some areas, but the government maintained control of the majority of the country. The factions' struggle over contested territory raged on for years.

In Barcelona, the coup initially seemed to be succeeding, with most of the officers stationed in the area supporting it. But a militia formed of local workers, unions and socialist splinter groups ran to the aid of the civil guard and mounted a counterattack. They manage to defeat the coup, but it took a horrific and bloody battle on the streets of the city to do it.

When Pawel and Stefan joined the International Brigade in the late Autumn of 1937, Franco's forces were already being supported by Hitler's German military machine. The city of Guernica had already been bombed by the German Luftwaffe. This was an international war. With German and Spanish Fascists fighting on one side and a collaboration of international troops on the other, it was a microcosm of the Second World War, which would follow quite soon after it. And it was a very different conflict to the one Zarec and Josef had fought in. There was no one front where everyone was fighting. Instead, there were pockets of fighting going on everywhere. Madrid was a year into a twenty-eight-month siege, and it was there that Pawel and Stefan were deployed.

It was going to be a real baptism of fire for both of them. Nothing in their young lives could have prepared them for the ferocity and brutality of war played out on the streets of this crumbling but once great capital city. They witnessed, terror, carnage and death on an industrial scale. People lived in bombed-out shells of their former homes, with a patchwork of splintered roof timbers teetering over their heads, and holes in the floor. Whenever there was a lull in the gunfire, lines of displaced refugees, clutching onto whatever they could lay claim to, seemed to pop up from nowhere. In a matter of seconds they would crowd the previously abandoned streets in all directions, pushing prams and wheelbarrows filled with random household effects like lamps, paintings and ornaments. Where they had just come from, or where they were all headed, was a mystery. After a few weeks, it was something Pawel and my father had grown used to, like the piles of corpses on the street corners after a bombing raid. The bodies just lay there, limbs limply suspended in the air, waiting to be gathered up and disposed of. Any romantic notions they'd once had about the war had been dispelled; this was the reality of what they had signed up for, and there was no going back.

Pawel and Stefan both had very different attitudes to authority. Pawel was quite happy to be told what to do. Following orders, fitting in, being a comrade in arms all came quite easily to him. He was also very physically fit, big and strong, so he was put in charge of quite a bulky, heavy machine gun. Like his grandfather before him, he quickly marked himself out as promotion material and was made a corporal. Stefan's transition from miner to soldier was not so easy. Initially, he was very much out of his depth. It was one thing to write home and impress women with talk about spending a week on your belly with a dagger between your teeth. To actually do it, and without an admiring audience, was something quite different. Stefan's natural desire was always to be noticed. On a battlefield, that is the last thing you want to be. Pawel, the consummate father figure, took him under his wing, kept him close and out of trouble. He managed to keep him alive long enough for my father to become the sort of person you need to be to survive as a soldier on a battlefield.

Another alienating factor for Stefan was that the other people in their platoon were all French, albeit a couple of them of Polish ancestry. He could not understand anything that was said without Pawel translating for him. This really got in the way of bonding with your comrades in arms. In the early months, if the rest of the boys were having a laugh about something, Stefan was constantly having to ask Pawel, 'What did he just say?' It's bizarre, but for my father to learn French, it took his leaving France and going to Spain.

Meanwhile, back in Les Baudrat, my mother was going into labour. I would like to say more about that, but accounts vary. When my mother recounts the tale, she describes a horrific ordeal lasting forty-eight hours. My granny, however, who was with her throughout and who delivered all the children born in that house, believed it to be one of the easiest childbirths she had ever seen. We will never know. All I do know is that at 4am on the morning of 21st January 1938, with Nadia and my granny at my mother's side, I came into the world and started a whole new generation in our family history.

Pretty much as soon as I was born, there were small indications that my mother and I did not bond as we should have. Every family is different, I know, but in ours Jasia and Mira had been not just the only girls in the family, but the babies of the family too. As such, they had had a very different upbringing to their brothers. They had been much more indulged, by both their parents and their brothers. Having a baby was the first bit of responsibility my mother had ever had in her life. If she had been living on her own, maybe she would have found her own way. Being dropped in the deep end can do that. But living at home with her mother, her sister and her unstoppable sister-in-law, it was far too easy for her to delegate the chores and responsibilities of looking after a baby to those around her. In the first couple of months after my birth, she was apparently struck with an illness that had them all confused. She would frequently spend whole days at a time in bed, where she would not want any food and would complain of feeling ill. She had no discernible symptoms, like a temperature, just an overriding feeling of fatigue, a lack of motivation and general aching. This sometimes resulted in her sleeping for over fifteen hours a day.

From a modern perspective, we might describe what she was going through as postnatal depression, but this was not something anybody in our household would have ever heard of back then. The family improvised and supported her in the best way that they could, and the preferred solution was simply to let her get on with it. If she wanted to sleep, let her sleep, maybe she was exhausted. If she didn't want to eat, don't give her food. In the meantime, the responsibility for looking after me was split between Nadia, granny Alinka and Mira. Even Michiek did the odd stint.

Josef was by now a very old man, in his 90s. He was still mobile and active for his age, but Alinka was having to help him dress and undress, see to his toileting and all the tasks associated with caring for someone elderly. She probably could have done without the extra responsibility of a baby. There were now eight mouths to feed, eight sets of clothes to wash, dry, iron and repair (and no washing machines back then, not even any indoor plumbing). Baskets of clothes were carried down to the stream, where a timber-framed hut with a red-tiled roof served as the village washery. My mother, my granny and my aunties would take turns to make that trip. They would dip dirty clothes in the stream water, rub them with soap on a flat stone, then rinse them and wring them by hand before taking them home to hang on the line. When I was older, I used to help. When clothes got worn out or damaged, popping out to buy new ones was never on the cards. For all her shortcomings as a parent, this was my mother's calling. From quite a young age, she had been the family seamstress. She was a natural with a needle and thread or with a set of knitting needles. Even our neighbours would come to her when they needed anything tricky done, which proved to be a useful revenue stream for the family when money got tight during the war.

With all of this going on, the notion that anyone could be tied up all day watching a young child was for the birds. As soon as I was old enough to crawl, let alone walk, I was just left to roam, like a feral animal. Not that I was likely to come to any harm. There was no traffic on the roads, and everybody in the neighbourhood knew who I was and where I lived. So off I would go. Every now and then someone would come out into the garden to dry some laundry or get some veg from the allotment, or maybe Michiek would come home from his shift at the mine, and they'd find me sitting in a flower bed, covered in mud, with a handful of leaves or invertebrates of one kind of another. They would pick me up and carry me back into the house. Receiving a quick brush down and a flurry with a wet flannel to get the worst of it off my face, I'd wriggle and shake my head, spitting and spluttering in protest. Then, as soon as I touched the floor again, I'd just toddle off to re-start my little adventure from wherever I'd left off.

*

Autumn 1938 and I was still in my first year. The family were getting ready for the winter by making preserves from whatever fruit they had been able to harvest. Meanwhile, news was starting to reach us that things in Spain were not going well. The Republicans had lost control of northern Spain, which had been their stronghold. Madrid had been reduced to a sea of rubble but somehow had still not yet fallen. My father and Pawel had been taken out of the urban battlefield and redeployed on the banks of the river Ebro in the Auts mountains of Aragon, northeast Spain. No one could have known at the time, but this was going to be the start of the longest and bloodiest battle of the Spanish Civil War. It was also going to be the death knell of the Republican effort to suppress the Nationalist uprising. By the end of the battle, Barcelona would fall, and millions of refugees would be marching north to France for shelter. Pretty well all the Republican senior military staff and politicians, who were meant to be leading their troops in battle, fled to exile in France alongside these refugees. The war was lost. When the Nationalists marched into Madrid to seize control of the national administration, they met no resistance.

Morale was horrific amongst the International Brigade and their fellow Republican troops. They were getting more and more despondent and demotivated by the day. Eventually Pawel and Stefan decided that their situation was too precarious and they too headed north for the French border; neither wanted to stick around to find out how they would be treated by the triumphant Nationalist forces. They set off in November 1938, and within a month had passed through Barcelona and made it to the French border near Cerbère. In the pandemonium of refugees trying to find shelter and safety, the two men, brandishing their French passports, were just waved through. They would be home in time for Christmas, and they wrote home to tell everyone the great news.

They got to us the week before Christmas itself, and it was the first time I ever saw my father and the first time he had ever seen me. He lifted me up in the air and spun me round and round and hugged me tight. He was over the moon. For the weeks that followed, he barely let me out of his sight. He took me everywhere, played with me, engaged with me. It must have seemed pretty weird to me at the time, as it was so different to what I had been used to. All the same, I don't think I would have objected. He was even there to see me take my first steps, a prospect that at times must have seemed vanishingly unlikely, while fleeing the Nationalist advance a few short months before.

I was not in a position to notice, but everyone could see a big change in my father. The man who returned from Spain was very different to the man who had gone out. He had lost a lot of his swagger and arrogance. He was still a show off at heart though. He could not help flaunting a revolver he had brought back from the battlefield to all the men in the village, firing off rounds in the street to impress them all. That incident aside, however, people who knew him observed a much more introverted man, less fun than he had once been. Even when playing with me, he would play largely in silence.

Christmas came and went, and suddenly it was 1939. For our family, life, it seemed, had gone back to normal. My parents and I moved back in with my father's family, and luckily feelings towards my mother had changed after my birth. The awkward, stifling atmosphere that had once prevailed there was now gone. Even Anetka opened up to my mother a bit, and they soon became friends. Pawel and my father went back to work in the mine, where they were heralded as war heroes or good socialists, depending on your point of view. For a while, life was good – even for me. An adoring father and an attentive grandmother was a big change from what I had been used to. As loving as my granny Alinka was, she had always been rushed off her feet and had little time to give.

I think everybody hoped that, from now, this was how things would be. The new normal. But world affairs were about to catch up with us again. A man we had never heard of in a country hundreds of miles away was making plans that would affect me and my family in the most dramatic of ways.

The Day War Broke Out

Barely a year had passed since Stefan and Pawel had returned home from Spain when the warning shots heralding the start of the Second World War were fired. The family reeled in horror when, in September 1939, Poland was invaded by both Nazi Germany from the west and Stalin's Soviet Union from the east. Poland was split in half by these two powerful neighbours, bringing back terrible memories of recent Polish history. Every evening both households would sit around their wireless to hear about further developments, and every day there would be more losses in Poland, and the prospect of war in France would seem more likely. My father sat in silence in his house, Pawel sat in silence in his, as news reached us of a frantic and valiant effort to suppress the German advance: Polish cavalrymen, mounted on horseback and brandishing swords, charged German tanks, predictably sustaining horrific causalities as a result. The desperation and the futility of this act summed up how impotent the people of Poland felt against the advance of the two great powers. Like many of their contemporaries, both Pawel and Stefan knew what a modern war looked like. Neither was in a hurry to relive their experiences, but the imperative to stand up to these old enemies was overwhelming.

In response to the invasion of Poland, France had declared war on Germany. The call had gone out for volunteers to bolster the armed forces, but coal miners, deemed to be essential workers, were discouraged from stepping forward; after all, the war machine could not operate without coal. However, as 'heroes of Spain', Pawel and

Stefan had inspired a lot of their circle of friends, including Michiek, and there was talk of little else down the pit.

By the end of September 1939, the French Saar Offensive in southern Germany had failed and the French army were having to retreat back into the Low Countries. By 6th October, Poland had surrendered completely and was once again partitioned between Germany and Russia. This was a rallying cry that no one could ignore, and in Montceau alone, vast queues of men formed up in the town square, ready to enlist. Pawel and Stefan finally succumbed to the peer pressure, and by the end of October 1939 they and all their immediate circle had enlisted together in the French army. I was still only one year old.

Michiek volunteered as well, but failed his medical, meaning he could not be deployed to front line duty. However, as an electrician (a rare skill back then) he was snapped up for a role in headquarters, where he would work on communications and be a key part of the war effort. Stefan, Pawel and the others were sent off for training before being deployed for action in Belgium. By now Josef was in his 80s, too old for any role; meanwhile Zarec, in his fifties, might have been too old for active duty but still had some more years left to give to the mine.

I sobbed bitterly that my father had no sooner come into my life than he had disappeared again. My mother was noticeably unsympathetic. As far as she was concerned, it was her loss not mine – a cruel and selfish way of looking at her daughter's distress, but one which, sadly, pretty much sums up my mother.

The new recruits from Montceau only had a few weeks' training, their commanders desperate to get soldiers to the front line as quickly as possible. Their first deployment was Belgium, and it would culminate with the last stand of the French in the Second World War. 15th May 1940, the Battle of Sedan: German troops were trying to push through Belgium. The allies believed that the Meuse River and the Ardennes mountains would be impenetrable for the German tanks, but within a month, not only had they managed it, but they had also pushed France and the Allied forces out of Belgium completely. The broken Allied forces retreated back as far as the northern French coast, where they were totally surrounded by the advancing German army. Both the French and the British forces were facing total annihilation, and Stefan, Pawel and the miners from Montceau were right in the thick of it.

There is a little-known peculiarity of a battlefield: soldiers spend long periods of their time just waiting around doing nothing. If anything, it gave you plenty of time to consider your position. The battlefields of Belgium stretched for miles. Despite the flatness of the landscape, the French lines stretched out of sight in both directions. Pawel, Stefan and their friends were all serving together in the same company and were dug into trenches facing a similar network of German trenches on the other side of a vast field. And all around them was still.

Then the distant rumble of artillery fire presaged a barrage of explosions around the French positions. Between each boom from the big guns came the *crack* of small arms fire, occasionally peppered with the sound of a machine gun. But it was all in the distance. Pawel and Stefan, battle-hardened from their experiences in Spain, were used to this, but their rookie friends soon grew frustrated.

'Surely we should be over there, where the fighting is?' one of them blurted in desperation. 'What use are we to anyone here? The war will be fought, and we won't have fired a single shot.'

Pawel took a long drag from his cigarette and looked the soldier in the eye. 'Don't you worry about that. The war will come to you soon enough.'

A few more hours of inactivity passed, and suddenly, as if someone had flicked a switch, there was a whistle in the air above them and an explosion in the middle of the field ahead of them. The NCOs sprung to life and started barking orders to the trench 'Take cover! Make your rifles safe! Stay down!' More shells fell, each one getting slightly closer to Pawel and Stefan's trench. The men hunkered down around them. One shell landed only a few meters away, showering them all with falling soil and rocks. Then, from behind them, more deep booming sounds started up, as the French guns started to return fire. This round of explosive tennis went on for some time. Every now and then a German shell would hit its target and a portion of the trench would explode. Men, guns, fragments of boxes, clothing and splinters of wood from the trench wall burst into the air, indistinguishable from the mud and rock which went up with it, falling and scattering the ground like a fan around them.

'Take your positions!' came the order. The men straightened and pointed their rifles over the top of the trench in the general direction of the opposing side. Pawel and Stefan hefted their rifles, even though there was nothing visible to take aim at. The others saw them and followed suit.

'Fire!' came the order, and all of them let off a volley of shots.

'What should we be aiming at?' someone asked.

'The Germans!' yelled Stefan, gesturing generally ahead of himself.

'I can't see any!' came the reply. A bullet whistled, striking a timber in the wall behind them, blasting splinters of wood into the air .

'They can't see you either. This is how it's done!'

Stefan turned, reloaded and opened fire again. His terrified comrade wrestled with the loading mechanism on his rifle, managed to load it, release the safety catch and began firing.

On a battlefield, the difference between a new recruit and a seasoned soldier is that the new recruit is still under the impression that there is sense to be made of it all – that there is a fragment of logic they might grasp that could help them overcome their fear of dying, help them to fight and survive. Pawel and Stefan were long past that. They knew that it was all a case of 'If you throw enough mud against a wall, some of it will stick'. In other words, keep firing in the general direction of the enemy, and eventually one side will run out of bullets, food, or bodies.

All the men saw of their enemy that day was the occasional flash of sparks as a rifle was fired in their direction. This carried on for two days, then just as inexplicably as it had started, the German attack stopped. The men stayed in their trenches for another day, then they were told to move out. They gathered their belongings and their weaponry, marched north to another set of trenches a few miles away. Then the whole cycle started all over again.

Back home in Montceau everyone was on tenterhooks. The nightly wireless broadcasts were not just about the fate of France. They contained the fates of people we knew and loved. And the news was very rarely good. It all got so hopeless so quickly. When my father and Pawel had been in Spain, there had seemed to be as many gains as there were losses, at least in the early days. This time it was just defeat after defeat after defeat.

In the early part of the war, even though my mother and I were living with my father's family, we would always spend a few days a week with my mother's family. Stefan's family were not regular churchgoers, so my granny insisted that my mother catch a bus across town every Sunday morning so she and I could go to Mass with the family. It was a highlight of the week for me – travelling by bus was a rare treat! Even better, we would normally have the bus to ourselves. When I was very little I would sit on my mother's lap and stare out of the window as we travelled to Les Baudrat. More latterly I would sit by a window on my own and she would sit in a different part of the bus completely.

The route used to take us over the canal bridge, and I would always look out for an old lady who would sit with her herd of brown goats as they grazed on the steep grass bank where the canal had been cut into the land around it, near the village of St Vallier. In later life I read Philip Larkin's poem 'The Whitsun Weddings', in which the poet recounts a train journey through the canal-cut countryside of Lincolnshire. Passing a cricket match, Larkin muses to himself that, just as the bowler released the ball, the match disappeared out of sight, so he will never know what happened next. This poem always brings me back to this old lady. Who was she? Where did she live? What did she do when she was not with her goats? I always had a very enquiring mind, something I think I inherited from my granny Alinka.

We would arrive at the house in time for my mother to catch up on the events of the week. I would busy myself playing in the garden if it was dry, and then we would all walk together, along with the rest of the village, to the little church. There would be so many of us it would look like it was bursting at the seams.

The congregation was pretty much all women, children and old men. Even though the miners were deemed essential workers, virtually all the middle generation of men from Les Baudrat had enlisted. For my granny's generation of women, the thirty-minute build up to Mass was like a piety competition. The winner was the old lady who could curtsey, kneel, cross themselves and mutter the most before the dull, resounding *bong* of the church bell signalled that Mass was about to begin, and everybody rose to their feet in a chorus of creaking wooden pews and floorboards. I cannot put my finger on what it is that I used to find so magical about a Catholic Mass. For me it was never about religion, as odd as that sounds. In a church as full as ours would be, there was a sense of theatre about the whole thing, and I think that was the appeal. The monotone and indiscernible rumble of congregational responses to the priest's pale tenor voice, the hollow echo of every sound under the high church roof, the spectacle of the priest in his robes so full of colour and jewels, the air thick with the smell of incense and the chorus of hymns with so many voices... It used to make the hairs on the back of my neck stand on end.

After Mass, Granny Alinka would walk with me in her arms to show me to all her friends. The nods of 'Oh how you've grown' and 'How old are you now?' varied little week to week, but I used to love it. Then we would all walk home together. My mother, Aunty Mira, Aunty Nadia and Granny Alinka would busy themselves getting food ready, Mira and my mum would be sent out into the garden to gather in the vegetables, while Nadia and Alinka would scrub every surface ready. Then the four of them would set about preparing and cooking lunch. They would barely come up for air from talking. Zarec would be sitting in a corner somewhere, sullenly ranting to himself about something. It was very difficult for me to know what he was always so upset about. His sentences would usually start in Polish, then would drift off into German, with a few French and Russian words dropped in, plus some others that could not be identified by anyone. Suffice it to say that once he went off into one of these rants, he was left to get on with it.

I would occupy myself with whatever I could find as a distraction or would bounce on my great grandpa Josef's knee. Lunch would normally be ready about 3pm. We would eat, talk some more, then everything would be washed, put away, scrubbed down and dried. And still the talking would go on.

The only interlude would be when the evening news was broadcast. The family wireless would be turned on in plenty of time, as the valves needed to warm up before you could hear any sound. Then we would all listen intently to every detail. When it was over, an uncharacteristic silence would prevail, as everyone absorbed what they had just heard. Then conversation would resume: what was happening in the war? What might come next? As there were no buses on a Sunday evening, my mother and I would stay overnight in Les Baudrat, and I am sure that conversations would go on until the small hours, long after I would have gone to sleep. Usually, on the Monday morning my mother and I would catch a bus back to our house, and on arrival conversation there would immediately start up with a further discussion of the last night's news.

Then on 25th June 1940 the French surrendered. In Montceau everybody held their breath. What did this mean for Michiek, Pawel, Stefan and the others? Were they even still alive? It was a very tense few days, with everybody desperate for updates but relatively little information coming through. First to arrive home was Michiek. His corps had been stood down immediately and sent home – the last thing the Germans wanted was French service personnel running their communications. But there was a delay in frontline troops returning, as it was not clear which parts of the army were going to be stood down and which were going to be maintained as instruments of the new German-controlled administration.

Eventually Pawel arrived home in Les Baudrat. The sight of him without my father had everyone in tears, partly in relief for Pawel, and otherwise in devastation that Stefan was still missing. My mother and I might have lost a husband and father respectively. Everyone hugged Pawel when he walked through the door of our house, like pilgrims touching a religious relic on a passing procession. He virtually had to peel them off in order to sit down at the table. When the wailing and weeping had subsided, my grandmother built up the courage to ask, 'And Stefan?'

Pawel shrugged his huge shoulders. 'I honestly don't know,' he said. 'We were fighting together but we got separated during the defence of Dunkirk. I haven't seen him since.' After a brief pause, to allow his family to digest this, he went on. 'He's reported as missing, not dead. So there is still hope.' But a look around that room suggested that hope was more in demand than in situ.

Days and days went by, and we heard nothing until, eventually, one day, my mother received a letter with an Edinburgh post mark. The envelope was frayed where it had been opened and read after sending, an indication of the sort of intrusion we were all going to have to learn to accept as part of life in an occupied country. The message the letter brought, however, quickly compensated for any anger at this violation. Stefan, my father, was alive. And he clearly had more lives than a cat.

His platoon had been dispatched into the dunes near Dunkirk. Their mission was to clear the area of German gun emplacements, to limit the German's ability to fire on the beach. It was a much harder task than had been anticipated. Carrying equipment over sand dunes is hard enough, but all the while they were under heavy fire from German infantry, and the Luftwaffe were dropping bombs on them from above. Every time they made any progress, they were swiftly pinned down and pushed back again, and soon they inadvertently found themselves cut off from the rest of their platoon, and on the beach itself. They re-grouped and found that their commanding officer was dead, so they formed up on the first line of dunes above the beach and fired inland. Pretty soon they realised that they were totally surrounded, and they had already lost most of their numbers; in a last fling of desperation, they shimmied down the dune onto the beach and made a run for it. They found themselves amongst a large contingent of French soldiers who were hoping to get evacuated out to England on board the flotilla of boats that were rescuing the British forces. Most did not make it, but somehow Stefan managed to blag his way on. He and three other men from his platoon found themselves on a tiny little boat so full of British and French service personnel that it could scarcely float above the waterline. But despite all the odds, it sailed with its crew and band of rescuers far enough out to sea to meet a Royal Navy frigate, which then sailed on to the English coast. There it docked. All those on board were met and catalogued by officials from the Admiralty, then taken to a camp for a cup of tea and biscuits to await further orders. Stefan was there for a few days, watching as those around him were moved on. The first to be moved out were the injured, who were taken to a field hospital that had been set up nearby. Then one by one the British servicemen were re-deployed back to their units until all that remained were non-British personnel. That was pretty well all French and Belgian soldiers, but fatefully, in Stefan's billet, it also included a survivor from the Polish forces.

Having fought with the French army, Stefan and the others had only heard news about the French campaign. Stefan had no idea that, despite Poland surrendering to the German troops on 6th October, a brigade of Polish soldiers had formed a Polish free army that was fighting alongside the Allied troops. They had been based at Anger in the Loire alongside the French troops, but France's capitulation after Dunkirk meant that the Poles very quickly had had to get out of France and head for the UK. General Sykorsky would now be running both the Polish government and its forces from exiled headquarters in London. The Polish army would be stationed in Scotland, ready to fight alongside the British. This was a revelation to Stefan, and when the British naval officer came to him with orders to report for duty in London with the French free army, his first action was to put in a request to transfer to the Polish army. His transfer was accepted, and the next thing he knew, he was on a train to Edinburgh with orders to report to the camp commandant as the latest recruit of the Third Polish Infantry Brigade. He was alive and well, and ready to get on with the war.

Everyone was ecstatic at the news. What a turn up! And there was particular pride that he was with the Polish army too. Somehow that just seemed right, although in truth the family had previously had no idea that Poland still possessed an army. Once the initial euphoria had calmed, however, a real cocktail of thoughts and emotions passed through everyone's minds.

I was far too small to understand what was going on, but I was naturally delighted to know that my father was alive and well, and I know I shared that with his parents and sister and my aunty Mira. But for my mother, there was a bit of emotional transitioning to contend with. Once the initial feeling of relief had subsided, she gradually began to question what he was playing at. When he had volunteered to fight in the Spanish Civil War, she and everyone else had believed it was because he really loved socialism. Then he had volunteered to fight for the French army and, now they had been defeated, was immediately putting himself forward for a second crack at the Germans with the Polish army. She began to wonder that it might be just that he really loved wars – or that he would do anything not to spend any time with her.

Such concerns didn't trouble Alinka and Josef. They were very proud that Stefan was now wearing a Polish military uniform, and in far better circumstances than Josef and Zarec had worn theirs during the pointless war against Czechoslovakia. Stefan had always talked a good game; now he was putting his money where his mouth was, facing down fascism by whatever means he could. No, their worries weren't with their son in law, but their son. It was clear that the cogs were silently spinning in Pawel's mind. He and Stefan had been through so much together; all he could think about was how he could get out there and fight alongside his friend and comrade. I am sure Nadia was all too aware of this, but uncharacteristically she said nothing.

It was less than a week later that we saw our first German soldiers in Montceau. A fleet of lorries with outriders and armed vehicles poured into the centre of town and cut their engines. The silence that followed was only broken by the sound of foot soldiers scurrying into position. First a file of them appeared, running down either side of the convoy and taking positions in shop doorways and on the street corners all the way along main street. An officer, flanked on either side by eight soldiers, marched up the steps of the Hotel de Ville. Two of the soldiers turned and stood guard at the top of the steps outside the door, whilst the others went inside. Half an hour later, the officer emerged from the main entrance, yelled something in German, and suddenly soldiers from two of the trucks disembarked and spread themselves out around the square. Two very smartly dressed officers then climbed down from their vehicle, were saluted by the one on the Hotel de Ville steps, and the three of them went back inside. The two empty trucks left the convoy and parked in the square, and then the whole convoy started up its engines again and rolled out of town. The convoy seemed to go on for miles and miles. No one had ever seen so many vehicles. But everybody knew that, from now on, things were going to be very different.

Where we lived, we were only a few miles down the road from Paray-le-Monial, the border with the *zone libre*, where the territory of the newly installed Vichy administration began. We, meanwhile, were in occupied France, and at the time we thought that there was a world of difference in that short distance. Little did we know that the zone was free only in name, in reality just an extension of Nazi-controlled France. I never really understood why they bothered with it. Everyone knew it was not truly independent or free. Why not just admit that all of France was occupied and be done with it?

There were some attractions of the ***zone libre***, however, and one of those was that there were less troops monitoring your movements. It was obvious that the window of opportunity to cross over the border was quickly closing, and it came as no surprise the following morning when Nadia, first to rise in their household, found a note on the table. Pawel had slunk off in the dead of night, no doubt wanting to spare himself the grief he had received when he'd volunteered to fight in Spain. He wrote that he was to meet up with a handful of men from the village, and under the cover of darkness, they would move through the countryside to cross the border, avoiding the roads and railway or any other area that might be easily guarded or patrolled. Once on the other side, the plan was to get to London somehow and join Stefan. There was not a lot of detail in the note about how they proposed to do this. Nadia read it, put it down on the table and got on with her daily chores. She must have seen it was coming, and she had no choice other than to be resigned to it. This, I think, explained her unusual reticence on the issue.

Pawel's journey, as you might expect, was going to be a fairly hairy one. There were six of them in total, and six men walking together in the direction of the border was too obvious. So the plan was that they would split into twos. The first pair would walk to Chalon-sur Saone, a nearby border point; another pair would move through woods to Gueugnon, and then head south along the Loire to Digoin; finally Pawel and his friend Henrick would head to Paray-le-Monial. The plan was to then meet up at a town called Lapalisse, which was roughly halfway between Paray-le-Monial and Vichy, soon to be declared the capital of the so called ***zone libre***. A man who lived there, and who had served in Henrick's platoon, had discussed meeting up and trying to get back into the fight, and they hoped to pick him up along the way.

Pawel and Henrick's journey would begin hidden on an empty barge heading south down the Canal du Centre as far as Volesvres. They would go the rest of the way on foot through fields, planning to cross the border at night. Of the six of them, only Pawel and Henrick were successful in making it. Though the German occupation of the area was still quite fresh, the German soldiers were very well prepared to deal with any groundswell of resistance, and their patrols covered much more ground than the men had anticipated.

Once across the border, Pawel and Henrik kept going, partly on foot, partly on the back of horse-drawn trailers on which they were able to hitch a ride. When they got to Lapalisse, they headed straight to their comrade in arms' house.

His wife answered the door. Rather a stern woman, she stood on the threshold of her doorway with her arms tightly folded and her lips tightly pursed.

'He's already gone,' she announced, once the two men had explained who they were. 'He went days ago.'

'To London?' enquired Henrick.

'London? How in the hell would he get to London?'

Pawel and Henrick exchanged glances, feeling quite uncomfortable that this whole conversation was taking place on the street, where anyone might overhear them. They felt like two little boys asking their friend's mother if he could come out to play.

'He's gone down to Marseille and got on a boat to Africa,' she added, 'and if you see him, tell him not to bother coming back.' And with that, she turned and closed the door on them.

The rather dumbfounded Pawel and Henrick went to a nearby café for a drink and to think about their plan. There were no Germans visible anywhere on the streets, so they felt quite easy about talking to a table of locals about their plans. However, at the mention of going to London, the men just laughed.

'Good luck,' came the reply, and it soon became apparent that the Germans were more than ready to frustrate any attempt they might make.

It turned out that, if they wanted to get to England, they had been heading in the wrong direction. No, in the opinion of the locals, their best bet would be to get to a port on the west coast, and the nearest was probably Bordeaux, over 400kms away – as far away as it was possible to be while still remaining in France. Moreover, the port was sure to be especially well guarded. And even assuming they could get on a boat, there would then be the crossing to England to contend with, across the Bay of Biscay, notorious for storms, and contested by the German navy, which was intercepting any vessels it could.

However, an altogether more viable alternative was to head south to the Mediterranean. The Vichy administration was responsible for France's colonies, which at the time included Morocco and Tunisia, and there were still regular crossings from Marseille and Toulon to ports on the North African coast. Once in North Africa, all they would have to do would be to move east, to where the fighting was, and re-enlist. They could always transfer to the Polish army at a later date.

So that is how Pawel and Henrick ended up in Tunisia, where, until the national surrender, French troops had been engaged in a battle with the Italians. The Italian army had since moved on towards Libya, and would then move onto Egypt, where they would meet up with German troops commanded by Rommel. They were now engaged in battle with the British and Commonwealth forces. The French free army, commanded from London by General de Gaulle, were already fighting alongside the British in this campaign, and it was to this action that their friend had gone. Within a week, they had made it to Libya, were re-enlisted back into the French army and were back on the battlefield once more.

In the last three years Pawel had fought on the streets of Madrid, in the mountains of northern Spain, on the plains of Belgium, on the beach at Dunkirk and now in the deserts of Libya. Never in his wildest dreams as a boy in Bardo could he ever have imagined even seeing any of these places, let alone fighting in all of them. But even though he was back fighting alongside many of his old comrades, Stefan was over 2,000 miles away in Scotland. Would their paths ever cross again?

Home Front

I was too little to appreciate what was going on at the time, but the changes France underwent as an occupied nation were immediate. Germany needed French coal to power her battleships and supply ships, so of all the things to become scarce in Montceau, suddenly local coal supplies were running low. Food supplies were erratic too. Some days the shops ran out of everything. Whispers would spread through the town if a shop was expecting a delivery, and by the following morning, a queue would be stretching down the street in anticipation.

But the scariest exemplification of this new, changed world came one Easter Sunday.

While my mother and my father's sister, Anetka, had not hit it off at first, as time went by, they warmed to each other. It was always a bit of a love/hate thing, but that was hardly a surprise: they were living together, and were a similar age, and also they were both vacuous dolly birds. But this last factor, at first the cause of their hostilities towards each other, latterly proved to be unifying.

My mother and I were still in the habit of getting the bus across town on a Sunday morning to visit my granny and the rest of the family, and as it was Easter Sunday, the invitation had been extended to the rest of the household. As I have said before, my father's side were not a churchgoing family, so initially Anetka and her parents said no. But my mother worked on Anetka, saying it would be a great opportunity to dress up in their prettiest clothes, and as there were not many opportunities to do so, in the end the idea swayed her.

So it was that on the morning of Easter Day, she and my mother dressed themselves up to the nines, as if they were going to a ball. When I stepped onto the bus with the pair of them in tow, fully made up, scarves flowing behind them and reeking of perfume, I felt like Cinderella with her stepsisters, even though I was in my special Easter dress. The bus driver was particularly impressed with the two of them, and flirted outrageously for the entire journey. They responded with a lot of giggling. I ignored them. I was too busy wondering if the old lady with the goats would be on the canal bank on Easter Day. She was. And as it was a sunny morning, she had a big-rimmed, black straw hat on to keep the sun out of her eyes. What a turn up!

We got off the bus at Les Baudrat. I ran ahead to see my granny as quickly as I could, my mother and my aunt tottering behind me, gingerly balancing on their high heels – not an easy thing to do when you're navigating cobblestones! The pair of them looked like stilt walkers.

You would never know there were food shortages from the sight that greeted me when I entered the house. Our table was creaking under the weight of plates of food, covered and ready for the feast after Mass. In the kitchen there was a lot of scurrying around. Alinka, Mira and Nadia all gave me hugs and kisses. Granny Alinka lifted me onto her hip and looked at me with those warm, smiling eyes. 'You look so beautiful,' she said. I could feel myself smiling back at her so hard it made my little cheek muscles ache. She picked up a wooden spoon from inside a bowl on the kitchen surface and gave it to me. It was the wooden spoon she had been using to mix cake ingredients with. She winked and said, 'I saved it for you.' I held the spoon by the handle and licked at it like it was a lollypop. There were some scraps left in the mixing bowl too. She set me down on the floor and I reached above my head to take it down off the side and cradled it under my arm. I set at it like a bee collecting nectar. To this day, I am certain that raw cake mix on a wooden spoon tastes so much better than any cake I've ever eaten. And my granny's cake mix was especially delicious.

My mother and Anetka made their entrance, swelling with pride at the gasps of admiration.

'Oh, what beautiful ladies!' said Nadia.

'Where did you find the silk?' asked Mira, never one to miss a detail.

To her credit, my mother didn't simply look good in clothes, she could make them well too. It is with some reluctance that I have to admit that she was probably the inspiration behind my own bent towards clothing design. Not that she ever encouraged me – she never encouraged me to do anything – but if I try to remain objective, I suppose that it is from her that I learned how clothes would hang if you cut or stitched them in a certain way – and that, after all, is how I made my subsequent career.

The little church in Les Baudrat was so full that day that anyone who arrived later than half an hour before the start of the service had to stand on the steps outside. As with any service where numbers are swollen by people who do not normally go to church, there was a certain tension in the room. Many attendants had to look around themselves to know when to stand, when to sit, when to cross yourself, when to mumble... A lady at the end of a pew at the front of the church raised her hand with some urgency to scratch a troublesome itch on the back of her head, and a third of the people sitting behind her instantly sprang to their feet, then just as quickly sat down again when they realised it was a false alarm.

During the service we prayed for the soldiers who were still at war for the mother country. A lot of uncomfortable glances were exchanged. Then at the end of the Mass we all walked back to the house, my mother and Anetka trailing behind the rest of us, pretending to be shocked by wolf whistles or coy about the compliments paid to them by men on the street.

When we got home the covers were pulled off the plates. Mira, Nadia and Alinka had made some creative use of garnish to make it look like there was a lot more than there really was. It was all part of the illusion of normality which everyone was trying to portray. For

Alinka it was doubly important, as she was desperate to give Anetka a good impression, so she would pass on to her own parents what an impressive spread of food had been laid on.

The rest of the day followed the usual pattern. When I had finished eating, I helped gather the things off the table, then ran out into the garden to play. It was a nice enough day. There were patchy clouds in the sky, but the sun was shining. I met up with some friends from the neighbourhood, and we played out in the street, out from under the feet of the grownups. Then at around 5, because it was still only March, the air turned cool, and we all went inside. The vodka had been flowing, and everyone was in good spirits. There was a lot of laughter and conversation and enthusiastic gestures, and as I walked in, Zarec, in a rare moment of jollity, smiled, pointed at me and said, '*Monia nina dupa*,' which means 'Monia who doesn't have a bottom'.

I looked quite shocked at this and replied, 'No, I've got a bottom. Look!' Then I turned around and lifted my dress and showed them my pants. The whole room collapsed in hysterical laughter, proper side-splitting belly laughs.

I was really unsure what was going on. My family didn't usually express themselves in such a joyous way. Even my mother seemed to appreciate it, 'Oh, Monia, you're so funny,' she said, laughing. This is probably the only time I can remember my mother saying anything bordering on a compliment. I suppose there must have been other occasions, but none spring to mind.

'*Monia nina dupa*,' Mira repeated through the uncontrollable laughter.

Bang on cue, I turned around and lifted my dress again. 'No, I've got a bottom. Look!' Once again, rapturous hysterics erupted.

Looking back, this memory is one of the happiest I have of my early years. Everybody was so joyful, everybody laughing, and I for once was the centre of everyone's attention. I was the cause of the hilarity, even if I had only managed to accidentally stumble on to that moment of comedy genius. I think I must have repeated my trick a dozen or more times before it was my bedtime. Every time it got the same reaction. I went to sleep with a beaming smile on my face.

The next morning there were a few sore heads around the kitchen table, but everyone was putting a brave face on it. After lunch my mother and Anetka decided that they would catch the next bus home.

'Are you sure you won't stay for dinner?' pleaded Alinka, in the full knowledge that there was no dinner.

'No, no, we must get back so I can wish my parents a happy Easter,' said Anetka.

So, with my mother and Anetka carrying their ridiculously impractical shoes, we walked down the street to the bus stop to wait for our lift home. A man I didn't know came over to talk to Anetka. They had met outside the church the previous day and he was very keen on her. He smiled and talked to her, leaning casually against the bus stop with his hands in his pockets. She blushed and acted coy. Then as the bus rounded the street corner she stood up and kissed him on the lips. His eyes nearly dropped out of his head. My mother tutted disapprovingly. We climbed on to the bus, Anetka stooping to wave at him through the window. He enthusiastically waved back, clutching the cap off his head to his chest. She sat down next to my mother while I sought out a window seat and we headed home. Neither of them exchanged a single word with each other for the whole journey.

At the bridge over the canal, there was a moment of disappointment for me. I couldn't see the herd of goats on the bank. *I wonder where she is?* I thought. Then, just as the bus reached the far side of the bridge, I could make her out, just about, a little further along the bank than usual. I sighed with relief. I didn't know what I would do if I ever crossed that bridge and she was not there.

When we arrived back at our house, it was immediately apparent that something was not quite right. Anetka called out, 'Mama! Papa!' but there was no answer. We looked in every room, in the garden and the cellar, but they were nowhere. It was obvious from the fireplace that no fire had been lit in it the previous night, despite it having been a cool evening.

'Where do you suppose they are?' my mother asked.

'Search me,' replied Anetka.

But strange as all this was, no one was worried at this point. The two of them set about getting things ready for dinner that night as if nothing were amiss. There were a few leftover potatoes and cabbage leaves and some cured belly pork in the larder, and they began making a stew. But time passed by and there was still no sign of my grandparents, and as the light began to dim, Anetka lit some paraffin lamps. Suddenly there was a knocking at the back door. Anetka and my mother looked quizzically at each other. No one ever came to the back door. It only led out into the garden. The two of them went to answer it. I waited at the doorway of the kitchen; I could sense that something was not as it should be. They opened the door to find one of our neighbours, a Polish man who worked with my father in the mine at Saunvigne, shuffling nervously from foot to foot.

Ashen faced, he said to us, 'You must go. You cannot stay here. It's not safe.'

Anetka and Jasia looked at each other. None of this was making any sense. 'What do you mean?' asked Anetka.

'Come with me,' he said, beckoning to us and nervously moving away down our garden. We closed the door behind us and started to follow him. 'No!' he said urgently. 'Go back inside and put those lights out.'

My mother turned and ran back into the house. We watched through the windows as she turned off the stew she had been preparing, then each of the paraffin lamps. Then she appeared at the door, closed and locked it behind her and ran into the garden. The man led us off, over the garden fence, which my mother had to lift me over. We ran through the garden of the house behind us. The couple who lived there stood by their window, arm in arm, sorrowfully watching our progress.

The man led us a few doors down the street that ran parallel with ours, then into the back garden of that house and knocked on the door. It was swiftly opened and we all bundled into the house, the door slamming closed behind us. By this point we were all quite frightened. Inside the house there was a group of three men in ***blue de travailles*** – blue work overalls – sitting around a table with glasses of wine and lots of bits of paper in front of them. The room was thick with the smoke of many cigarettes. There was also a very frightened-looking woman. I had never met that woman before in my life, but when she saw us, she ran to me, scooped me up off the ground and held me tight. I could feel her sobbing through her tight embrace. The men who were sitting at the table stood up, cleared away the papers and beckoned my mother and Anetka to sit down. We had no idea at the time, but these were men of the Maquis, the French resistance.

'What's going on?' my mother asked.

There was a pause as everyone exchanged glances. After a moment, one of the men, a gruff, ruddy-faced miner with puffy cheeks dotted with pox marks and a big bushy moustache, stepped forward. 'Your parents… they came for them yesterday.'

'Who came for them?' Anetka demanded.

'German soldiers,' came the reply. 'Gestapo,' added another.

Both women gasped. 'What? What do you mean? Why would they come for them?'

There was a long, drawn-out silence. Eventually the man we had followed across the garden asked calmly, 'Have you got somewhere you can go? Somewhere safe? Away from here?'

'Yes,' my mother answered.

'Where?' he enquired.

'My family have a house in Les Baudrat.'

'That would be perfect. Do you know anyone with a car?'

My mother and Anetka shook their heads.

'Then you can stay here tonight. The little girl can sleep in a bed in the front room. Tomorrow morning you will have to leave. It's not safe for you here.'

I could sense from the expressions on their faces that both my mother and Anetka had experienced that dull thud you feel in the pit of your stomach when you realise that you are currently undergoing something life-changingly bad. It was a feeling I could recognise; I was experiencing it too. The lady who had been holding me handed me to my mother and led us both into a dark, quiet room. Neither of them said anything, but as my mother laid me down on the bed, I could see tears forming in her eyes. They both turned and went out of my room, pulling the door without closing it. From my bedroom I could hear Anetka and my mother sobbing and crying in the other room, Anetka constantly repeating, 'I don't understand! I don't understand! Why, why why?' the lady trying to give them soothing words, the three men talking over each other.

The next morning my mother woke me. She and Anetka both looked like they had been up crying all night; their eyes were bloodshot, with dark rings round them. It was such a contrast from the exuberant glamour they had exuded only a couple of days earlier. The lady gave me a piece of bread and a glass of milk for my breakfast. Then we set off for the bus stop, my mother and Anetka looking at the ground the whole way there. As far as I am aware, we never went back to the house, not until after the war. We moved into the house in Les Baudrat with my mother's family and took nothing more with us than the clothes we were standing in.

We had no idea why the Germans took my grandparents away. Apparently, that night they had rounded up lots of people. Some were Jews, some journalists, some communists, and lots of other people who did not seem to have any obvious label. Just like millions of others like them, right the way across Europe, they disappeared without trace or explanation. It was the final sign, as if another had been needed: we were completely powerless. Once again, the fate of my family had been decided on the whim of someone we had never even met.

The early days after my grandparents' disappearance were very raw for us. Most of the family tried to avoid the subject unless either my mother or Anetka brought it up. I don't think my mother could get her head around the fact that it had happened at all. In her mind it was as if it were all just a big misunderstanding, and any minute now, they would walk through the doors with some rational explanation. Anetka was also rather stunned, lunging from moments of sadness accompanied by uncontrollable sobbing and wailing, to seeming to take it all in her stride, able to talk about it all in a detached, objective manner. She slept a lot during the day but could not sleep at night. It was obvious that she was very stressed, highly strung. It was not just that her parents had disappeared; it was the fact that it would be impossible to get closure. There would be no funeral, not even the certainty that there ***should*** be a funeral; there were no dead bodies, after all. No one dared to ask the police or the authorities for information, in case that only led to the disappearance of Anetka and Jasia as well.

A couple of months into our new life, Anetka developed a grey streak through her hair that ran from her fringe to her crown. Vain as she was, she went to great lengths to hide it. Hair dye was quite hard to come by in the war, and when it wasn't available, she would try to make her own, using whatever she could lay her hands on to do the job. I thought it looked funky, but I guess funky wasn't the look she was going for.

No one had explained to me what had happened, not in terms I could understand. I could see for myself that my grandparents were not at the house and that no one knew where they were. I also had some inexplicable third sense that told me that it was not something I should ask about. So I didn't, not until I was much older. And when I did, all I learned was that no one was any the wiser than me. It was a total mystery. But back then I was just as occupied by the old lady relocating her goats to a different stretch of canal bank. I wondered if there was any connection with that and my grandparents' disappearance. It is funny how a child's brain processes things.

Anetka, my mother and I stayed with the family in Les Baudrat throughout the war. It was a bit of a squeeze – no one in the house had a bed to themselves – but it was cosy. We got to pool our resources. We had Michiek and Zarec's wages coming in from the mine, Josef had a minuscule miner's pension, and Mira got a job at the munitions factory in Monchanin so we had her wage coming in too. To drum up some more income, my mother took in alteration and seamstress work. She had a great reputation in the village, and people happily paid what they could for her to recycle old clothes into new ones. When I got a bit older, I would help her, which meant that she had to teach me some of her skills. This was a rare bonding moment between me and my mother. Granny Alinka got a job cleaning for the local priest one day a week. For her it was a dream job, and one she was immensely proud of. And Nadia got some occasional work in the kitchen of the nearby Chateau du Plessis in Blanzy, where she learned some fantastic French cuisine, recipes which she brought home and cooked for us. As a qualified electrician, Michiek did work for people in the village, mostly shops, cafes, and local farmers. Rather than do these jobs for cash, which might not always be available, he would use a bartering system. Before long, everyone in the village owed him for work, which kept food coming in even at times when money could not have bought a crumb. Between everyone, we managed to keep ourselves afloat. We certainly fared a lot better than most of the other families in the village. We were a good team.

One team player I haven't yet mentioned was Anetka. I have said previously that she was very attractive, full of self-confidence and a bit of a flirt. I was far too little at the time to understand what was really going on, but even I could not fail to notice that Anetka seemed to have a lot of boyfriends. And she wasn't fussy. There were old ones, married ones, fat ones, Even the odd German one too. Growing up in Gdansk, of course, meant that she spoke German fluently. When I was a lot older, I remember overhearing Anetka and my mother having a blazing row, in which I learned from my mother more words for 'prostitute' than I could have imagined existed. I can't say for certain if Anetka was genuinely sleeping with men for money, or if this was just my mother being her usual cruel self. But either way, through her male friends, Anetka provided more than her fair share of fresh meat for the household. Especially around the time I would sometimes see her being led into the woods by the local butcher, her slim, elegant hand being clasped in his sweaty, stumpy, fat one.

As you might imagine, her relationships with husbands and, more seriously, German soldiers made her very unpopular with the other ladies of Les Baudrat. Granny Alinka, I am sure, would have been utterly outraged had she been outside of our household. But the war was a strange time, and as I said, we all came together as a team. So Alinka looked out for Anetka, and made sure that these tensions did not spill over into anything more serious.

Anetka's flirtations also made it possible for me to wake up one morning to discover that I was the hero of the village. I didn't have much in the way of toys when I was growing up. They were expensive, hard to come by and not our biggest priority. I did have a few wooden toys which my great grandfather Josef had carved for me with his pocketknife, and a few which my father had bought for me before going off to fight in the war. But by far my favourite was a little blue-and-red metal tricycle Michiek brought home one day. He had done a bit of work for a local farmer and spotted it gathering dust in the corner of a barn. The thing was ancient, having once belonged to the farmer's son, who was now grown up. But I didn't care. I thought it was amazing. I used to hurtle around on it, up and down the paths in our garden and along the pavement in front of our house, and I would feel like I was the queen of speed.

It was, however, a frequent source of beatings from my mother. I was always forgetting to put it away again, once I had finished playing with it. It was supposed to be kept in the cellar, out of the way, not cluttering up the garden path. Sometimes, if it was getting dark, I would be afraid of going into the cellar; more often than not, though, I would simply forget to put it away.

On just such an occasion one evening, a couple of German soldiers had stopped by the house to chat over a cigarette with Anetka. It really was nothing more than that. Whatever it was Anetka used to get up to, she never got up to it in the house. When the time came for Anetka to return indoors, the soldiers set off on their way, to continue with their patrol. But after taking no more than one or two paces, there was a cry, a crash, and what I can only assume to be some choice German swearwords. One of the soldiers had accidentally stepped on the tricycle, and his weight had sent it shooting out from under his foot, sending him flying through the air and down the steps of our cellar, where he landed awkwardly and painfully on his back. He also managed to break one of his legs in the process.

The shouting and swearing brought people running out of their houses to see what the commotion was. Between them, they managed to lift the German casualty of war to the top of the stairs, every now and then giving a surreptitious nudge to his broken leg. After a while, a military ambulance came and took him away. I was fast asleep through all of this, so when I woke the following morning, I was blissfully unaware that my beloved tricycle was smashed to pieces. But over breakfast it was all anybody could talk about, and the gravity of what had happened only really started to sink in as I walked to school. Normally that walk was quite uneventful. I would skip along the pavement, singing to myself or roleplaying some game in my head. But on this day, I was absolutely dumbfounded to find everybody I passed smiling at me. Most of them even clapped or cheered! Total strangers were coming up to me and giving me sweets or money!

In school all the teachers had heard that I was the little girl who had put a German soldier in hospital with my tactical placement of my tricycle at the top of the stairs to the cellar. All day long they were coming up to me to congratulate me and say well done. Then when I got home, there was a crowd waiting for me with a brand new, shiny tricycle that the people of the village had clubbed together to buy for me. I was the hero of Les Baudrat!

Poles Apart

The year leading up to my fifth birthday was an eventful one to say the least.

I had started school and had developed my own little circle of friends beyond just the kids who lived on my street. To help me blend into a French school, my family thought it would be a good idea if they told the school that my name was 'Monique', the French version of Monia. I'm sure they did it with the best of intentions, but it made my first day at school even more stressful than it needed to be. I didn't just have to contend with going somewhere new and intimidating, trying to fit in, trying not to get lost, and trying to remember the regimentation of it all; I also had to remember that I had a new name. I had to introduce myself to people using it, and to make sure I answered to it when it was called. I coped well enough, but looking back it seems a little unnecessary – it's not like I was the only Pole in the neighbourhood!

By now I was old enough to help with tidying up and clearing the dinner table after meals, and picking vegetables from the garden for dinner. I did my bit on the home front, which made me feel quite proud and important, like one of the grownups. When I had time to myself, I was starting to explore two interests that absorbed me thoroughly. The first was nature and the second, rather intrinsically linked, was drawing. There was nothing I loved more than combining these two hobbies. I would sit for hours in the garden or in the fields or woods, drawing flowers, trees and insects. My mother said that my drawings were rubbish, but my granny thought they were great. She used to proudly hang them up in the house for all to see, and as it was her house, there was nothing my mother could do about it.

I was also starting to form my own interpretations of the people and things around me. My newfound enlightenment had led me to notice that my mother was not like the mothers of my friends. They always seemed to be kind. They would smile when they spoke to me and ask how my family was. They would also show an interest in me and the things I said or did. They would ask what I was drawing. They would ask to see my drawings. They would ask how I was enjoying school. My own mother never did any of those things. And even looking back with the perspective of an adult, it is still quite difficult to make sense of why. It is also just as difficult to be dispassionate about it. As a child, all you want from a mother is love and security. Being deprived of those obviously has practical implications, but on a personal, emotional level, it just really hurts. And not just at the time. To this day, it is capable of bringing a lump to my throat, a tear to my eye.

I think my mother had enjoyed being the baby of the family: having all the attention, having everyone dance around her, doing things for her, looking out for her. She always seemed resentful about having to grow up and do things for herself. She was also very jealous of anybody who ever got the kind of attention she wanted. She was jealous of me for now being the baby of the family and usurping the focus of affection from her mother. She was jealous of Anetka for attracting more attention from men. She was even jealous or Mira for being a younger sister. These things used to really bother her, and she would express this jealousy in the cruellest of ways. To be fair to her, she had also been the victim of abuse herself; it was unfortunate for both of us that she seemed to have inherited her father's cruelty and violent temper. She would give me beatings over the most trivial of things. I remember once I was sitting in the garden, drawing, when she came out through the front door of the house. She saw me sitting there, quietly minding my own business, came storming over to where I was, grabbed me tightly by the arm, lifted me up and dragged me into the house. I was already crying, partly from the shock, partly from the fact that she was hurting me, and partly with anticipation of what was coming next. She stood me by the kitchen table and yelled, 'What do you think you are doing? Lazing around in the garden, drawing your stupid pictures! You are a lazy waste of time! There is work to do in the house. Do you think I should have to do it all? Do you? Do you think it is my job to clean the house and you can do nothing?'

By now I was sobbing my heart out, but this only seemed to enrage her further.

'You are wasting the day with your stupid pictures! If you've got time to be doing that, then you have time to help me clean the house. And now I am going to give you something to help you remember that!'

'No!' I pleaded, but with that she took a belt off a hook and frantically whipped away at me with it. I put my hands and arms up to protect myself. She grabbed them and held them down with one arm, and with the other did what she could to beat me with the belt. I screamed with every swipe. Drawn by my cries, my granny appeared, and running over to us, she took the belt out of my mother's hand.

'What are you doing?' she shouted.

My mother was by now red in the face with rage. 'Don't you interfere, you old hag!' she screamed. 'She's my daughter and I will deal with her how I see fit!'

'What has the girl done?' my granny shouted back.

'She's a lazy waste of space! She does nothing to help me. I'm left to do all the work in the house and all she does is waste her time on her stupid drawings!'

'You've only just got out of bed yourself! This girl has done nothing wrong. Get out from here!'

And with that, my mother stormed out of the house yelling Polish profanities as she went.

I was beside myself, not just from the pain, not just from the humiliation, but because it seemed that my mother hated me. I didn't know why, and I didn't know how to make it better. I just felt hopeless, useless – alone and lost. I felt like it must be my fault. My granny hugged me in an effort to comfort me, but I was inconsolable. Even when I had managed to quieten myself down, I would still break out in fits of sobbing for the rest of the day. Even now, when I think back on that incident, I can feel myself filling up. She *had* only just got out of bed herself. What a cow.

This was not an isolated incident. It only stands out in my memory because of my granny's pointing out of the total injustice of it. My mother had just wanted to beat me, and when asked to give a reason, she blurted out the first thing she could come up with. Just like her own father, it never occurred to her to consider such things; all that mattered was her own supposed grievance.

What if I had that same gene? What if I had it in me to be so cruel to my own child? To be so hurtful, so hateful, so damaging? I remember thinking back on my childhood a lot when I found out that I was expecting a baby myself, and these questions played very heavily on my mind. I knew how much my mother's parenting had messed me up. What if I was doomed to repeat the same mistakes? But I was equally worried that, even if I was able to stop myself from becoming my own mother, I wouldn't know how to behave in order to be a good one.

It may sound like an odd thing to say, but when my mother wasn't beating me or being hateful, the rest of my family life was enjoyable. Life in Les Baudrat had become settled. Since the disappearance of my grandparents, everyone had got used to living in one house, and to managing without Pawel and Stefan. We had all settled into our own roles and routines.

The German occupation was by now part of everyday life. It influenced who in the village we could and couldn't talk to, where I was and was not allowed to play, which shops we could go to, which ones we should avoid. Everything had got pretty tribal amongst the locals in Les Baudrat, and seeing German soldiers patrolling the streets or asking to check your papers in town or on the bus was a regular occurrence. On the surface, people seemed to tolerate it all as part of everyday life. Beneath the surface, however, they were seething. The only acceptance they had come to was the fact they were powerless to do anything about it.

But it's not as if we were all resigned to it. There were resistance fighters in the village. The identities of the Maquis were closely guarded secrets. They had supplies and weapons dropped in by the RAF under cover of night, and they frequently ran sabotage missions around the coal mines to scupper the supply of coal to the Germans. Despite all the secrecy that surrounded these people, however, somehow everyone seemed to be in the know when something was about to happen. All the grownups in every house in the village knew that for the next couple of days we were not to play in a specific wood or near a specific road. We would be warned to stay away, and sure enough, somewhere in that window of time there would be an incident, an ambush or an execution.

There was one incident I recall very well. The maquis did not usually detonate bombs, and the horrific consequences that seared this episode into my memory perhaps explain why.

There was a little girl at my school. She also went to our church. Her name was Maja. She was a couple of years older than me, but no more than eight or nine. She was very pretty and had a beautiful singing voice. She was given a solo to sing in church that Christmas. She lived on the opposite side of the village to me, so we were not close, but she always seemed very sweet and kind whenever our paths crossed.

A lane meandered out of the village through some woods, and on the other side of these woods there was a field which regularly held three or four horses. Maja used to love horses, and she liked to walk to that field to feed them apples and pet them over the fence. On this particular day the resistance had planted a sizeable bomb under the winding gear of the lift at the local pit. It had been supplied by the British. The men who worked at the pit knew to stay away from that shaft, and to Maja the lanes must have seemed oddly deserted. For whatever reason, she either had not got the message, had forgotten about it, or had chosen to ignore it. We will never know which. When the bomb went off, it was with such force that steel struts and supports and the winding gear at the top of the tower were blown apart, and the jagged fragments of steel and iron showered into the surrounding countryside. Maja must have been scared out of her wits. First the bang of the explosion, sending the horses in a crazed dash for safety, then the shards of steel and iron raining down from above.

When she was found, she could only be identified from her clothing. At her funeral her casket was closed. Heaven only knows what the tiny body in that box must have looked like. All the horses in the field were killed as well.

That the was the truth of life under occupation. While there might have been no visible war around us, we were never far from death. It never escaped me how easily it could have been me in that casket. I used to walk down that lane with my friends all the time. I used to draw the horses in the field. I had once given Maja one of those drawings and she had seemed delighted with it. My friends and I had used to make dens and play 'house' in the woods, and we would pretend that the field where the horses were was our stable. That game just never seemed appropriate after that day.

Most people could tell you that war broke out in 1939 when Germany invaded Poland. A detail that tends to get overlooked, however, is that her then ally the Soviet Union also invaded Poland from the east at the same time. Then in June 1941, out of the blue, Hitler launched a surprise attack on the Soviets, supposedly her ally. Stalin was furious, entering into a new treaty with Britain and agreeing to fight alongside them against the Nazis. He mustered the full force of the Red Army against Germany, creating an eastern front. As you can imagine, Churchill, the British and her allies were delighted with this. Britain had been getting more and more isolated in the war, and this was exactly the sort of break they needed if they were going to turn things around.

However, one particular political thorn made this changing of sides more than a little awkward. As a result of Stalin invading Poland in 1939, there were thousands of Polish troops languishing in gulags and labour camps across Russia and Siberia. Churchill, encouraged by General Sikorsky, urged Stalin to release these Poles, so that they might be deployed in the field. If Stalin had been a different sort of leader, no doubt this request would have been accepted without argument. But he knew perfectly well that some pretty dark deeds had been carried out on the Poles, both during the invasion and their subsequent incarceration. Reports of these depredations would not endear him to his new allies in London. Accordingly, the Soviets deployed a lot of smoke and mirrors to make this request difficult to fulfil. The Poles already did not trust Stalin one inch, but the British were so desperate to keep the Soviets on side they did nothing to push the issue, even to the extent of accepting their denials of having large numbers of Polish prisoners at all. Then when the Soviets did admit that they had them, to ensure war secrets were kept close to home, they insisted that these Poles should be deployed into the Red Army, rather than receive the status of Polish free troops. Churchill, not wanting to rock the boat, initially agreed to this.

But pressure was now mounting on Churchill from two sides. On the one hand, Sikorsky was pleading with him to get his troops out of Russia, and on the other, Montgomery and his British generals were pointing out that a few thousand additional troops in North Africa would come in pretty handy. Churchill finally plucked up the courage to push the issue with Stalin. He suggested that if some of the Poles could be deployed in the Middle East and North Africa, that would be nice, but if Stalin wanted to keep the majority of them back to fight on the Eastern Front, then so be it. After some delay, Stalin reluctantly agreed, and under the command of General Anders, the eastern army and the Carpathian Brigade were formed. By August 1941 they had been deployed to support the British defence of the first siege of Tobruk on the Libyan coast, where 35,000 Germans and Italians under the command of Rommel fought tooth and nail with 27,000 British and allied troops for nearly four months.

Coincidentally, this was also where Pawel and Henrick had ended up. All along, their plan had been to transfer at the earliest opportunity from the French to the Polish free army. The arrival of this large Polish contingent of the Carpathian Brigade gave them the opportunity to do just that. They would still be fighting alongside the British and under British overall command, but as Poles rather than French. They knew this fact would make their families proud.

The Poles of the Carpathian Brigade had forged a very distinctive character as a fighting force in a very short space of time. And nothing encapsulated this character more than their mascot. Having moved south from Russia, across the Middle East, to end up in North Africa, they had passed through Iran. Here, they had stumbled upon a Syrian brown bear cub whose mother had been killed by hunters. They rescued it, adopted it and, more latterly, they kept it as a pet. It went with them everywhere, including into battle. Wojtek, as he was named, ultimately became not just their mascot but also the regimental emblem of the Polish II Corps. He pretty much embodied their ferocious and cavalier approach to desert fighting. The men of the Carpathian Brigade were used to being poorly equipped and fighting with outdated technology and weapons. Many had survived incarceration in totally inhospitable conditions in Siberia. As a result, they were much less reliant on supply lines and conventional approaches to warfare. They were very resourceful, masters of improvisation.

One particular incident, which escalated into a diplomatic ticking off, serves as a great example. Some Polish airmen had been sent out on a bombing raid from the RAF base on Malta. After they had dropped their payload on their target and were returning to base, a German camp was spotted below. They had no more bombs to drop, and they did not have enough fuel to double back or change altitude, so all the men on board dropped their trousers and squatted over the open bomb doors, evacuating their bowels over the enemy. Like I said, resourceful. They must have hit their targets, because apparently, despite all the atrocities of the war, the German high command complained to the British authorities that this just wasn't cricket. By all means, drop bombs and annihilate hundreds of soldiers while they sleep in their beds. But having a pooh? That's just going too far.

The arrival of this new brand of soldier really lifted the spirits of Pawel and Henrick and those other Poles who were already in North Africa. And the quirky addition of Wojtek, the beer swigging, cigarette-smoking bear, made their arrival seem the stuff of legends. This is exactly what was needed. The siege of Tobruk was a protracted affair with some vicious fighting and very heavy casualties on both sides. Anything to keep the troops' hopes up was welcome. In the end, against all the odds, the British, Polish and Allied Commonwealth forces held the port, a significant victory for them.

Stefan, meanwhile, had been in Scotland for over a year and out of action for pretty much all that time. Some of the people he was stationed with had been deployed to fight in Norway, but for whatever reason, he personally never got called up to join them. He and his fellow volunteers who had yet to be deployed were desperate to get into the fight. But their commanders were reluctant to see them deployed on the Eastern Front, when North Africa seemed to be where they could be of most use.

Eventually they were mobilised, many to Iraq. Stefan, however, found himself in Egypt. Up to this point things had not been going swimmingly in the desert campaign. Any battle involving the Italians generally went the way of the Allies, but Rommel's German troops were of a totally different calibre, well equipped, and kept in supply directly from the Mediterranean coast. They controlled everything east of Malta.

It's quite hard to imagine what arriving in a war zone must be like. Especially when you stop to think about this particular war zone, and the men who were arriving there. These were men who had been brought up on the Baltic coast, a place synonymous with being cold; and they had just spent the last year either in Scotland or Siberia. Now they arrived into a desert in the full height of summer. And if that were not enough, some of the cream of Germany's army were waiting for them.

Neither was there anything you might call a bedding in period. The men were counted in, issued with weapons and ammunition and deployed straight to the defensive line. Fortunately, at this point fighting was infrequent in their part of Egypt, mainly just skirmishes, but no one was under any illusion. They knew it was just a matter of time.

Stefan and Pawel had both been made corporals in their respective companies. By now, of course, they were both battle hardened from previous campaigns, and their commanding officers were keen to exploit that. Neither had any experience of fighting in a desert, but during the defence of Tobruk, Pawel was able to draw on tactics he had learned on the streets of Madrid.

As I have mentioned before, the two friends had very different personalities, and both men employed contrasting approaches to their new responsibilities. Pawel, like most of the men on my mother's side of the family, quietly got on with the job in hand. Nothing really seemed to rattle him; he was a very calming influence on his soldiers. Moreover, he was also reassuringly strong, his physical presence making the people around him feel safe. His strength had practical applications too. He became the talk of the brigade when he and four other soldiers were patrolling a stretch of the ancient ramparts that surrounded the old port of Tobruk. The old town wall had been badly damaged by artillery fire and bombings, so you had to tread carefully. One member of the patrol lost his footing as some masonry broke loose from under his weight, and he started to fall through the air. Pawel swung out at him and caught him with one hand and lifted him to safety with a heave of his enormous arm. The rest of the patrol just stared on with mouths aghast. The men in his unit would do anything for Pawel, and they knew he would do anything for them.

Stefan was much more of a joker in his approach. He would be the one sending new recruits on pointless errands just to raise a laugh amongst the more seasoned men in his charge. All of the old favourites were utilised: 'Go to the quartermaster and ask for a tin of rainbow paint', or 'a left-handed pistol'... My father's banter made him popular, but in a very different way from Pawel. When the fighting started, though, he knew how to switch it off and be the professional soldier he needed to be. It was like a reflex with him.

By now it was the tail end of August 1942. The British and Free French were just about to meet Rommel at the decisive battle at El Alamein. Pawel and Henrick and their company had been dispatched to a desert camp just a few miles outside Alexandria in Egypt. It was a vast camp, made up of troops from many different companies. Some of them were Polish, some Canadian, some Indian, some New Zealanders, some Australian, some French but the majority British. You could get a clear sense of how global this war was just from this one camp.

Pawel and Henrick had been there for a couple of days and were taking a short cut back to their billet after a patrol when they faintly heard a familiar sound. Just audible in the still night air was the sound of an impromptu band. You could clearly hear the plucking of a banjo accompanying an accordion and a group of voices singing 'Hej Sokoly', a rousing Polish folk song that had been very popular with soldiers during the war against Russia. It stopped Pawel and Henrick in their tracks. They turned and walked towards where the music appeared to be coming from, a task made easier by the site of a flickering fire. No doubt that was where the singers were sitting.

They pushed through a small crowd who were standing around the fire. Some were onlookers, but most were Poles singing their hearts out. And there in the company of musicians, leading the singing, was Stefan and his trusty banjo. He seemed to be having a happy war. At first Pawel and Henrick said nothing. They just stood there in the crowd, waiting for him to look up and notice them. Then when he did, he flung his banjo to the ground, shot to his feet and ran to them, holding Pawel in a tight embrace. The two old soldiers were virtually in tears at the sight of one another; both had long since given up any hope of meeting up again until the war was over. The three of them stayed up all night, swigging contraband vodka that some light fingers had lifted from the officers' supplies. They had a lot of catching up to do. So much had happened in the two years since they had last met. And how appropriate it should be that what brought them together was the song, 'Hej Sokoly', which translates as 'Falcons Rising'.

The next morning both their units were moved out of the camp ready to face Rommel's German forces. They were not deployed together, but now they both knew which company the other was in, they were able to keep tabs on each other and stay in contact. They both wanted to write home with the fantastic news of their reunion, but to have done so would have been to put everyone at home in terrible danger. Instead they had to suppress the urge to share such good news and press on with their duties.

Pigs and Troughs

There was a little gang of us from school who went everywhere together. We played on the street, we played in the woods, down by the lake and around the wash house. We were inseparable. We were all in the same class at school and lived no more than a few streets away from each other. I was very shy as a little girl and didn't make friends easily. This was probably a by-product of having the confidence knocked out of me by my mother. But now here I was with a little gang, fitting right in and having fun. One thing helped: now I was old enough to make my own way to school, my mother had found a job with her younger sister, Mira, at the munitions factory. She was making shells that might be fired at her husband, but I'm not sure if she ever stopped to think about that; for her a job was just a job, another revenue stream coming into the house. And for me, it was freedom. Not having her around to criticise and chastise, I began to stretch my wings a bit.

We had plenty of games to play to keep us occupied. What the English call 'hopscotch' we used to call '*escargot*'. We would play it for hours. We also loved our hobby horses and skipping ropes (I was amazing at skipping) and of course games of house and hide and seek in the woods. Usually I would join in and play, but sometimes I would sit and draw my friends.

'Let's play war,' one of the boys would usually suggest. You would think that, having seen and experienced some of the ugly realities of war, this would have been repugnant to us. Not at all. In fact, we used to play it a lot. 'The boys can be the French and the girls can be the Germans!' he'd go on.

'That's not fair. You always get to be the French!' one of my circle would pipe up.

'No we don't'!'

'I don't want to be a German. I want to be French!'

In our games, the French always won, of course, and the Germans always all got killed. I remember one occasion when, immersed in our usual argument, we were oblivious to two German soldiers patrolling the street. Overhearing us, one piped up with some corrective history. 'But the Germans always win,' he said in perfect French. 'France doesn't even have an army anymore.' He smiled triumphantly at his challenge to us. We all stood in the street staring at him. I don't think he meant any malice by it. It was more than likely meant as a light-hearted observation. All the same, we were frightened of him. He was a German, after all. The enemy. And he had a rifle over his shoulder. But more significant in our minds was the fact that our families had told us that we were not allowed to talk to German soldiers. After a moment of exchanging glances, we all turned and ran as fast as we could into the woods. But even as we ran we were laughing. That led to the best game of war ever. We were all French this time, pretending to kill the real Germans patrolling our street by shooting at them with sticks and shouting 'Bang!' from behind the tree line. It was epic. I knew that my dad would have been so proud of me.

Nicole was a little girl I knew from school. She never fitted in to any gangs. In fact, she didn't seem to have any friends at all. I used to feel really sorry for her. These days she would be described as having learning difficulties. We have much more sensitivity around these sorts of things now. Back then, the kindest words I ever heard anyone use to describe her came from her parents, who called her a simpleton. The other children were much less restrained. Nicole was quite a bit older than us, around twelve or thirteen, I think; in France children who did not pass their year got held back to do it again. She was taunted and bullied something rotten. I seemed to be the only one who felt that this was wrong. It always seemed to be me who was left sticking by her or consoling her. I would try and comfort her until the teacher would come, but even they lacked the empathy and patience you would expect. I even remember Madame Berger, our form mistress, who usually seemed so caring, shouting at her, 'You're not crying again? For heaven's sake cut it out. Just stand up to those bullies or shut up!' As you can imagine, that did nothing to improve the situation.

I suppose I was the closest thing Nicole had to a friend, but only because I wasn't horrible to her. I knew what that felt like from my own mother. So, while she wasn't part of my little gang, I did sometimes go over to where she would be playing alone and offer words of kindness or encouragement to her. She would smile. She didn't really talk. She sometimes tried, but she spoke so slowly, and with so much of a drawl, that it was impossible to make any sense of it.

She nearly killed me once. I know that sounds dramatic but it's true.

A small river flowed near the neighbouring village of Gautherets, called the Bourbince. It was not a waterway of any significance. Its main function was to feed water into the Canal du Centre. It flowed through the principal mining areas in Montceau, so the water was always filthy with coal pollution. However, for me it was a great spot; there were always butterflies and dragonflies near the river, and on sunny days I used to love to walk down to the riverbank and draw them. Nicole was not allowed out on her own, but on the day in question she had come to Gautherets with her father, who was visiting a friend who lived in a house opposite where I was sitting. She saw me sitting by the river and came over to me. I looked up and smiled when I saw her. I showed her the picture I was drawing, and she smiled back. Her father called over to her. 'Stay away from the water. Do you hear?' She acknowledged him and just stood next to me, watching me draw. After a few minutes she sat down and for a moment all was peaceful and calm. All we could hear was the gentle sound of the water breaking over stones on the riverbed. It was quite a warm day so I kicked off my shoes and decided to paddle in the shallows of the river. That black, contaminated water must have looked inviting to me; I suppose if that's what you're used to, you don't question it. All the waterways around Montceau used to be black, so I grew up assuming that this was the colour rivers were meant to be.

Now I cannot be sure if Nicole got excited by my walking into the river or frightened that I might be in danger, but for some reason she got really agitated. At first, I just ignored her, but she kept it up, and I gestured to her to calm down. Then out of the blue she came bounding through the water towards me and had grabbed my arm. I was startled by this; I had no idea what she was playing at. I pulled back and struggled with her, shouting at her to let me go. But she held on, getting more and more agitated and upset. Then I slipped on the wet stones on the riverbed and fell into the water. With that, Nicole decided to sit on my chest. I think this was an attempt at humour, because she was laughing while she was doing it. I was flailing around in the water, trying to get her off, but every time I opened my mouth to shout for help, I ended up taking a mouthful of water. I could feel the burn of it choking up my throat and lungs. Nicole was heavy and strong. I don't know how long I was in the water for. All I can tell you is that I was literally moments away from drowning. I had almost blacked out when Nicole's father came running over. He grabbed Nicole and pulled her off me, then put his arm under my still and lifeless body and threw me onto the riverbank. I landed on my back and the impact made me cough up the buckets full of water I had swallowed in the struggle. I coughed and spluttered for a good ten minutes, fighting desperately to catch my breath. I was crying with the shock of it all. Nicole, meanwhile, was receiving the hiding of her life off her dad, so by now she was crying too.

He wrapped me in a blanket from his friend's house and walked me home to explain to my granny what had happened and to apologise. I was beside myself. I kept being sick. I was cold. Even after I had been dried off and put into clean clothes I could not warm up. I kept shivering. My throat and chest hurt from the strain of taking in so much water, and I was still lightheaded. The whole experience had been horrific, but its true horror did not surface for another week or so.

Over a week later, I was still suffering from a sore throat and feeling faint and lightheaded. A day came when I got sent home from school, so my granny took me to a nurse who took my temperature. I had a fever and the nurse suggested that I might have picked up a bug or a tonsil infection at school. She instructed that I should be put to bed, given some hot soup and wait and see how I was in the morning. The next day I was no better. In fact my condition had deteriorated. I was running a really high temperature; my throat glands were red raw and swollen; I was off my food, because it hurt to swallow; and I was having real trouble breathing. My chest still hurt, but everyone assumed that this was an aftereffect of having swallowed so much water. It got so bad that even my mother, in a rare moment of maternal instinct, grew concerned. It was agreed that the village doctor should be sent for. He owed the family a favour anyway because Michiek had done some electrical work for him.

The doctor's diagnosis was that I had contracted diphtheria. It's normally a tropical disease, but clearly it had come to Les Baudrats. As close to death as the near drowning had brought me, this would be infinitely worse. The condition these days is treated with antibiotics, but these were not available in any plentiful supply in German-occupied Saunvigne. The doctor gave me what he could, but the drugs he prescribed could only manage the symptoms, not cure them. I was fading in and out of consciousness for weeks. I felt somehow detached from reality, like I was inside a soundproof box, screaming to be heard but not able to make a sound. Whenever I did come around, my mother would be sitting by my bed, reading to me or soothing me or cleaning the sores which were starting to form on my skin. To this day, I cannot be certain if this was real or some kind of a hallucination.

It was so out of character for her. But it seems that maybe she did care about me on some level after all. Sometimes my granny would be there too, kneeling by the bedside, clutching her rosary beads and praying. I know she was doing this for the best of reasons, but it was somewhat unnerving. My throat and chest felt like they were tightly wrapped in barbed wire. I could barely breathe.

The symptoms had me in their grip to one degree or another for the best part of a month. I am very lucky to be alive. Once it had started to lift, the symptoms dropped away quite quickly, but I still had to stay isolated in my room as diphtheria is so contagious. It was a good six weeks before I could go out and play with my friends again. I was initially very angry with Nicole, as the whole episode had been so needless and so awful. But when I saw her again after the incident, I could not be cross with her. She was totally oblivious to her part in what I had been through. Her grip on the real world was a slender one at the best of times, and everyone else was so horrible to her, I don't think it would have helped anyone if I had started to be horrible to her too. However, being friendly was a step too far for me; I blanked her and walked past and kept my distance from her after that. Looking back on it now, I feel quite ashamed of that. I had lived through hell because of her, I know, but I had come out the other side and life was back to normal. Her hell, the relentless teasing and bullying, continued every day, without respite.

The experience of nearly losing me had changed my mother's attitude to me somewhat. The beatings subsided and she was a lot more reasonable, even affectionate towards me. As a child there is nothing more important to you than the love of your parents, particularly if it's something you have been deprived of. I was grateful for it but never took it for granted. I was still quite tentative around my mother; you cannot just erase all your memories at the drop of a hat.

The first time I went to Mass after being ill was a weird experience. The congregation had been praying for me every Sunday. Now my walking into church was like a visitation. You'd think they would have appreciated me as walking proof of the power of prayer. But instead they were incredulous. I kept catching people staring at me. It was as if I had come back from the dead or something. Clearly none of them had believed I was going to make it. It made me wonder: if they were so certain I was going to die, what was the point in praying for me? Surely you only pray with the belief that God will answer you? But this was a question I chose not to voice out loud. Our priest found being challenged very difficult to deal with, and would quickly get defensive, even if the person asking (usually me) was just innocently seeking clarification rather than trying to pick holes in their faith.

One person in church who was definitely ***not*** staring at me was my aunty Mira. She had eyes only for a local man called Jakub. She couldn't take her eyes off him. Unfortunately, she was not the only one. His family were Polish, he worked underground at Saunvigne, and not only was he rather handsome, he had the build of an athlete. He was an excellent footballer. So good, in fact, that after the war he was selected to play for Gueugnon FC. Gueugnon was just up the road from Saunvigne, not a particularly big place, best known for its steel works, but its football team, formed during the war, always punched well above its weight, holding their own against the likes of Lyon, Paris and Marseille. In 1947, Jakub would be a key part in their winning the Championnat de France Amateur. But at this particular moment in time, he just played for the local village side, which was not a team of any note. His skills were head and shoulders above those of his peers, so he was something of a hero amongst the team and their followers, a proper local celebrity.

Everyone knew that he and Mira had been seeing each other, but no one knew how serious it was getting. Then one day she came home in floods of tears. Everyone rushed to her, to comfort her, assuming that he had been a bastard and done something to let her down. But in fact, he had asked to marry her, and she was crying with joy. My mother looked scathing but everyone else was really happy for her. It was fantastic news.

As soon as wedding plans were in the works, Nadia was on the case. In her usual way, she would ensure that everything ran with military precision. Nadia was never happier than when she had a mammoth task to coordinate. Combine this with my granny's desire always to give a good impression, Mira was going to have the wedding of the century – whether she wanted it or not.

One difficulty would be catering for lots of people. We were, remember, under food rationing. The family put their heads together to come up with a solution. I have mentioned how Anetka would use her feminine charms to get us fresh meat from the local butcher. But what the family came up with on this occasion knocked that into the shade.

As I was still a little girl I was not included with this scheming. It was something the grownups hatched between themselves after I had gone to bed. So you can imagine my surprise when I came into the kitchen for breakfast one morning only to discover that we had a pig living in a pen in the corner! Once the initial surprise had worn off, I was absolutely overjoyed. I had always wanted a pet. A pig would not have been my first choice, but there was a war on, and you had to learn to take whatever you could get.

Michiek had called in some favours from the local farmer. He had done some work for him and this was to be his payment. This pig would give us enough meat to feed all the wedding guests, and we'd still have some left over for us. The only problem was that we had to smuggle it into the house under cover of night, feed it and fatten it up, slaughter it and butcher it ourselves, without alerting any neighbours or, worse still, the Germans to the fact that it was in the house.

You might think that keeping a pig in the kitchen would be unhygienic, but apart from toileting, the creature was very clean, and not smelly like you might imagine. He did sometimes get excited and start to grunt and whine when he knew he was about to be fed. But as he was such a creature of habit, we always knew to tie a hanky around his snout to suppress the noise. That pig was lovely. The family made me swear to secrecy, which was so hard: all I wanted to do was tell all my friends and show them our pig. I was so excited. It was agony saying nothing.

For a short time he became something of an obsession for me. First thing in the morning I would run over to say good morning to him and he would grunt back. I would feed him whatever scraps were left from the table and pat him and he would give me a satisfied grunt for my trouble. He was the first 'Hello!' I would shout when I came home from school or in from playing outside with my friends.

My family tried their best to let me down gently. One morning after breakfast, my granny lifted me onto her knee and looked at me very seriously.

'You know, Monia,' she said, 'the pig isn't a pet. We are going to need to slaughter it. It's food.'

'Yes, of course,' I replied. 'I know that.' The fact was I did know it. And given that we kept chickens and rabbits in the garden, which were routinely dispatched, you would think I'd have understood the real implications. But as much as I kidded myself, on some level it hadn't really sunk in.

Even my great grandfather, who was on his last legs himself, called to me from his bed to explain to me that I should not get too attached to the pig. 'Of course,' I said reassuringly. 'I know that.' Then half an hour later I would be sitting by his pen in the kitchen, stroking his snout through the bars.

Michiek came the closest to discouraging me. 'You have only just got over a terrible disease,' he said. 'You remember how it felt when you were ill?'

I nodded silently. I remembered all too well.

'Well keep away from that pig. They are riddled with diseases, and if you keep touching him, you will make yourself ill again.'

That did get through to me. I was still terrified by the experience of the diphtheria so, after that, I kept away from the pig.... for a few days. Then I went back to petting him. Only now I knew to do it in secret.

A Funeral and a Wedding

We soon reached the time when the pig would have to be slaughtered. But how to kill it without raising the alarm? Pigs are notoriously noisy when they are about to be killed; they have a sixth sense that alerts them to the fact that death is imminent, and they squeal the place down until the deed is done. But if our pig did this, we risked being shot. We had been told by the farmer that the best way was to finish it quickly, while the pig was distracted with some treats.

That, however, was only one of our problems, and I'm afraid the other was rather macabre: how to kill the pig without creating a blood bath? When you slit a pig's throat, an awful lot of blood gushes out, and if it is not contained it creates a horrible smell and all sorts of other issues, any one of which could give the game away. The farmer explained that usually the pig would have its legs bound together so it could be hung by those binds from a hook once the cut had been made. The blood could then be collected neatly in a bucket underneath. But this would not work for us. We were pretty sure that, if it suddenly found itself with its legs bound, the pig would know something was up. So we had to cobble together our own plan.

I say 'we'. I want to make it clear that I had nothing to do with what followed.

After much debate, the grownups decided to lead the pig down into the basement. Everyone was to play a part. Nadia would hold the rope around its neck, which they would use as a lead; Zarec would be executioner; Anetka would stroke the pig and speak soothingly to it so it would not get overexcited. Once it was fully calm, Zarec would swiftly cut its throat with a sharp knife, Michiek would slide a bucket under the cut to catch all the blood, while my mother bound its hindlegs in a pre-made noose; everyone would then lift the pig onto the hook in the roof and leave the bucket underneath to catch the rest. Brilliant. They'd considered everything. What could possibly go wrong?

As it turns out, pretty much everything.

To be fair, the first issue was one no one could have foreseen. It seems that our pig was scared of the dark. As soon as he was led out of the kitchen into the darkness of night, he started squealing. The grownups couldn't risk that, so they brought him straight back into the house, waited until sunrise and led him out early, before the neighbours were awake. This worked fine until they got to the cellar, which of course had no lighting. The pig started squealing again and had to be rushed back upstairs and back into the kitchen. Reluctantly, Michiek had to give up his weekend to spend it installing electricity and lighting in the cellar – all to keep the pig happy!

To make doubly sure that this time things would run smoothly, no one fed the pig that day; instead its feeding bowl was put down in the cellar ready. When he entered the cellar in the early morning light, he made a beeline straight for it, pulling poor Nadia to the ground and dragging her behind him. He was a much bigger and more powerful beast than anyone had really given him credit for. They had anticipated leading him to the bowl so that he was positioned directly below the hook he would subsequently be hung from. Instead he approached the bowl with a sweep round to the right, and was now standing at the wrong angle. They had to coax him into position by nudging the bowl. The pig was furious at this and made his feelings known with an angry squeal. Various members of the family tried to shepherd him, but he was just too strong to be led and too heavy to be pushed.

In the end, Zarec acted with his usual degree of sophisticated forethought and, rather than wait until the animal was in the right position, just cut his throat anyway. But his first cut didn't do the job, and the animal lunged forward squealing. Zarec pounced on him like a lion with a gazelle and was dragged around the basement by the bleeding, squealing animal He swiped again, and this time it brought the animal to the ground and made him fall silent. Now, however, he was spurting blood everywhere. Michiek ran over and tried to haul the pig over to the bucket, but the animal weighed a ton. My mother managed to get the noose over the pig's hindlegs, and pulling together, everyone managed to drag the animal over to the hook and haul him up with the rope. By now there were thick pools of blood all over the cellar floor, and pulling the animal up vertically sent blood spurting everywhere like a sprinkler. By the time Michiek got the bucket underneath the spray, everyone was drenched from head to toe in claret-red pig's blood. It was in their clothes, their hair, on their skin, their shoes... They looked like something from a Stephen King film. Yes, somehow they had managed to slaughter the pig without drawing attention to themselves, but now how on earth were they going to be able to go back upstairs without anyone seeing them? To make things worse, they could now hear me upstairs, getting up for school in an empty house.

Remember, I was not involved in this plan at all. It had all been cooked up after I had gone to bed. So when I walked into the empty kitchen, naturally I wondered where everyone was. 'Mother?' I called out. 'Granny? Aunty Nadia? Piggy?' There was no answer. I walked around the house looking for them. My great grandfather was awake but lying in his bed. From the noises he had heard coming up from the cellar during the early hours, he had a vague idea what was going on.

'Do not worry, Monia,' he said reassuringly. 'They have had to go out this morning. Just have your breakfast and be on your way.'

I did as I was told, trying my best not to ask all the questions that were buzzing around in my head. Secretly I think I had deduced that the pig was a goner, but I tried every way I could to try to convince myself that maybe he had escaped, and that all the family had gone to find him. It was just plausible enough, and far easier to accept than the inevitable truth.

After breakfast I trotted off to school in my usual way. For my family, stuck down in the cellar, this was one obstacle removed. But they still had a quandary: how to get out without being spotted? And then, how to deal with all the blood? If this disaster was to happen these days, you could deal with it easily enough. You would run a bath, bathe person number one, pull out the plug, give the bath a quick clean, then turn on the taps and bathe person number two. But in our house in the early 1940s, it was not so easy. To take a bath under normal circumstances, a tin bath would have to be placed in front of the stove while a couple of large pots were filled with water and placed on the stove to heat up. The whole family would take it in turns to bathe, and we would all share the same water. But with everyone drenched in pig's blood, that was out of the question.

In the end, it was decided that everyone would wait until the neighbours had gone to work, then one by one would emerge and go upstairs. Nadia would go first. She would have to see to great grandpa while heating water for herself to have a bath. Once she was clean, she would go down to let the next person know that the coast was clear, and so on. Michiek would be second as he was due in work first. After the two of them had bathed, the bath would be cleaned while fresh water was gathered and heated.

As you might expect, this took ages. By the time Anetka – bringing up the rear – had come up and bathed, it was mid-afternoon. She was not best pleased at having to spend the best part of a day stuck in a cellar with a dead pig, her skin and clothes stiff with its dried blood. Saturated beyond washing, everyone's clothes had to be thrown out and burned.

When I came home from school, I was oblivious to the horror show that had unfolded.

'Where's the pig?' I asked innocently.

A barrage of hard stares greeted me. Was it something I had said?

Nadia squatted down in front of me. 'Now, you remember why we got the pig, Monia?' she started. 'It was so we would have enough food, wasn't it?'

I slowly nodded, my little heart pounding, my eyes welling up.

'So the time has come for the piggy to go to sleep. Do you understand?' She was so calm and collected with her explanation, her voice so soothing in its delivery, but all I wanted to do was wail out loud. I ran to my room, buried my face in my pillow to stifle the noise and howled.

My granny came to me and stroked my hair until I was able to lift my head up. 'There, there,' she said, 'he's in heaven now, able to run and play with all the piggy friends and brothers and sisters he used to know before he came to us. He is happier there than in our kitchen.'

I was sobbing so deeply it made my whole body shudder, but I managed to say something that surprised everyone, not least myself: 'I want to see him,' I said. And if there were any doubt that I meant it, I added, 'I want to see him dead.'

My granny looked aghast. 'No. I don't think that's a good idea.' She knew perfectly well how attached I had grown to the pig. Understandably, in her mind, the last thing I needed to witness was the reality of the piggy carnage. I burst into tears again, punching the pillow with my fists and kicking the bed.

At this point my mother walked in. 'What the hell is going on?' she demanded.

Before my granny could answer, I blurted, 'I want to see him dead!'

My mother shrugged her shoulders. 'Well, let her see him dead then. She'll soon shut up after that.'

My granny frowned and gestured with her head that this was not a good idea. But it was too late. I was up on my feet, wiping away the tears and looking up at my mother. 'Take me then,' I said.

So my mother held out her hand and marched me off into the cellar. It's the strangest thing, but even though it was not a pretty sight, once I had seen him, I was fine. I can't explain why, or back it up with any psychological explanation. It's just how I felt.

All the things we try to shield our children from these days – nudity, sex, toileting, violence, death – these were all things I encountered regularly as a little girl. I saw the men and women of the family in the bath, I saw them using the potty, I shared a bedroom with newlyweds, I saw the corpse of a murdered pig. Even when my great grandfather died, he remained in his bed in the house for me to see before the undertakers took him away. And it wasn't just me. Back then, every working-class family – probably in the world – had children who were exposed to these things. The only people who did not see this stuff were the upper classes, who had houses big enough for adults and children to be in separate rooms, and had staff to take care of such messy business as slaughtering and butchering animals. For the rest of us it was part of everyday life. Do I feel that I was damaged by seeing all this? No, not really. Should kids be exposed to it these days? I suppose probably not all of it, but maybe our attitude to death, and our efforts to block out where our food comes from, have taken a step too far toward an over-sanitised world. After all, death is no less natural than anything else in life.

Having seen the pig's lifeless carcass I was now determined that the animal should have a proper send off. If my granny was right about him being able to go to piggy heaven (and I'm sure she was) then really, it was up to me to commit his soul to God. We couldn't exactly ask the priest, but with my granny's help, I didn't see why I couldn't manage it. After all, she was the most pious person I knew.

So the two of us kneeled down in the garden, near the entrance to the cellar, and said our prayers together, to commit the pig to Saint Anthony (the patron saint of pigs) and ask for God to watch over his soul. The rabbits and chickens eyed us up suspiciously from their pens, while my mother and Anetka stood by the steps to the house smoking cigarettes and silently sneering at us.

Nadia was pretty handy with a knife, and so she was appointed the butcher of the family. In no time at all the pig carcass had been cut and salted and packed. Now we were able to look forward to the more pleasant aspects of the wedding.

The whole neighbourhood had been involved in the wedding preparations in one way or another, so we asked a trusted few to store some food in their larders. The farmer who had let us have the pig offered up his biggest barn as the venue, and my mother stitched together tablecloths, bunting and wall decorations to make the place feel more homely. We and all our neighbours brought our dinner tables and chairs along, so there would be enough places for all the guests to sit, and Anetka came up trumps by laying her hands on enough bottles of vodka to keep all the guests going. No one enquired too deeply about how she had managed it.

As marriage is secular in France, on the day itself, the ceremony took place in the village Marie, followed by a blessing from the priest in our local church. Then it was onto the farm. I had never seen so many people; there were hundreds: all the Poles from Sauvignes and Gautherets, all the Poles from Jakub's family and friends, the football team and so on. The food production line was tightly orchestrated, with Nadia in charge of operations and a never-ending army of local women taking shifts to do their bit. Every adult had a jug of vodka and a glass in front of them. Children came dressed in Polish national costume, and a raucous time was had by all. This wedding went on for two days.

Before the wedding itself, I had not really had that much to do with Jakub. But he seemed nice, and when we were having our family photographs taken at the wedding, he held my hand and wanted me to be at the front. He said he thought I looked beautiful. I blushed. I think I may have had a little crush on him. He was great with us kids; still in his wedding suit, he even joined in a football match between me and my friends in a field next to the barn. He ran rings round us; no one could get anywhere near him, and it made us all laugh like drains!

We were unaware of it at the time, but as the party went on, he was getting more and more bored. He did not drink much, so hordes of drunk, droning old men, telling him about how he should play football, or what they had achieved on the pitch in their own youths, was not exactly doing it for him. At one point, my friends and I were playing under the tables, and we emerged near to where he was sitting. He caught my eye and came over to us.

'Hey,' he said, 'do you children want to make some money?'

'Sure,' we all replied enthusiastically.

'Then watch for my signal. If you see me wink at you, I want you to go under the table, come up where I am sitting and give me a plausible reason why I should go with you. Every time you do that, I will give you 20 centimes.'

'20 centimes!' we echoed excitedly. Imagine what we could do with all that money! My friends and I spent the rest of the party rescuing my new uncle Jakub from boring drunks. We all made well over one Franc each, a fortune to us, and one which perhaps gives you an idea of just how much he enjoyed the celebration.

A band of local musicians who my father had performed with were called to come along and play Polish folk songs. There was a banjo player, a drummer, a woodwind player and an accordion player who also sang. They played all the favourites for everyone to dance, sing along or cry to. Anetka and my mother led the singing, my granny smiled and tapped her fingers in time with the music, Michiek swung his glass in the air, and Zarec... well, Zarec engaged in his usual arguments with himself, muttering his displeasure with the world. He was just left to get on with it.

Obviously, us kids were not present at the party for the full two days. We had to go home to sleep, and our mothers came with us. But for the men, it was a straight forty-eight-hour session. Then it was up the next morning and off to work – though I doubt much got done that day.

Jakub was a foreman at the mine, quite a good position, and as Mira also brought in a wage, working at the munitions factory, they were the first in the family to move out and into a home of their own. This was the height of ambition and made my mother very envious (quelle surprise). It was a house very similar to ours, just up the road in Les

Gautherets. A whole house with just the two of them in it? It seemed so decadent! I loved that house. I would go and visit whenever I could, and sometimes stay over, especially when I was a little older. They had a bit of money so could afford to have all the mod cons. They were the first people I knew to have a telephone and a car, and after the war they got a fridge and a TV before anyone else as well. The family were definitely moving up in the world.

The Italian Campaign

The Battle of El Alamein resulted in a British and Commonwealth victory over Rommel, and seemed to herald a turn in the tide in the North African theatre. It led to a lot of political toing and froing on the Allied side as to what to do next. The Americans were pushing the idea of a large-scale deployment in northern France. But Churchill wanted to keep the fighting around the Mediterranean, 'the soft underbelly' of Europe as he referred to it. In the middle of all this was the tiny voice of General Sykorsky, the commander of the Polish free forces. He had his own agenda, which he was urgently trying to get heard.

By April 1943, the Nazi's campaign against the Soviets on the Eastern Front had run into difficulties. They had already lost the battle of Stalingrad, but despite that, they had managed to capture and hold some territories east of the Soviet border, including the area around Katyn Forest. There, they had found grisly evidence of one of Stalin's dirty little secrets: mass graves filled with the uniformed corpses of Polish army officers, massacred by the Soviets after they had surrendered. If they were facing reversals on the battlefield, here the Germans had a PR coup de grace: they could expose the Soviets for what they were, loosening the alliance between Stalin and the other Allies.

Twenty-two thousand Poles had been executed across Katyn and the prisons at Kalinin and Khariv. Most of them were army officers, but their number also included doctors, lawyers, journalists, police officers, teachers, priests and intellectuals. Naturally, Sykorsky was furious and wanted the Allies to launch a full inquiry into the matter. He also wanted to get the eastern Polish army out of Russia for their own safety. Churchill would do neither, refusing anything that might endanger the resolve of the Soviets to continue fighting the Germans.

Information about this atrocity was vitriolically pushed through all German-controlled news channels, including in France. As such, it also filtered down to the Polish troops in North Africa.

I remember vividly when I first heard the news myself. We were huddled around our wireless as usual, tuned into the BBC World Service to listen to the news being broadcast in French. If I ever hear the '*pom pom pom pom*' drum beat that was the overture to the BBC News, perhaps on a documentary about the war years, I still get goosepimples. It whisks me right back to those nights when the family huddled around, listening in silence: '*Allo! Allo! Ici Londres...*' through crackles and whizzing noises.

Normally, when the news was on, we would be totally silent for the whole broadcast; it was, after all, one of our few connections to the outside, unoccupied world. But on the day of the discovery at Katyn Woods, the rest of the broadcast was drowned out by horrified gasps and everyone shouting in disbelief. We just could not believe what we were hearing. I learned some really choice Polish swear-words, as Zarec pounded the table with his fists. He was ready to take the Soviets on himself that night.

The news really brought home to us our dilemma: who was on our side and who was against us? What does being an ally mean? The whole war had started because France and Britain wanted to defend Poland. Where was that resolve now? It looked like a pretty hollow promise in that moment.

Amongst the Poles in North Africa there was very nearly an uprising. Many of them had fought in the campaign against the Soviets alongside the men who had been massacred. Now they wanted to gather up their arms and march back to Russia to give Stalin a pasting. They were all incensed by the injustice done to their comrades. Their commanders had a devil of a job trying to keep them from deserting, especially when the news reached them that Churchill had refused to allow an inquiry. Hot heads in the searing desert made for a very volatile atmosphere at the best of times. From the commanders' point of view, it was important that the men were deployed into action as soon as possible. The longer they were left in the desert, the greater the likelihood of a mutiny.

Eventually the Allied commanders reached a compromise as to the next stage of the war. After victory in Africa was assured, the British would go along with the American idea of landings in northern France. Preparations for this plan saw the desert war heroes Montgomery and Eisenhower transferred to London. In the meantime, the Allies would commit a smaller fighting force to pushing north through Italy, to rout out the Germans and Italians around the Mediterranean. This, they concluded, sounded like a job for the Poles.

So it was that, in the wake of this diplomatic meltdown, the Poles from Scotland and the Poles of the Carpathian Brigade were once again split up. Uncle Pawel and his friend Henrick were with the Carpathian Brigade, fifty thousand strong and under the command of General Anders. They were sent to Palestine for training, ready for the campaign. Meanwhile, my father and his company were technically part of the British Eighth Army, so they found themselves being herded on to army transports ready to move out for phase one of the Italian campaign: Sicily.

A real hotchpotch of nationalities took part in this exercise, including Poles, South Africans, Canadians, Free Greeks even Brazilians ready to cross the Mediterranean in British and American ships, ready to link up with the Italian resistance on the other side. No one knew it at the time, but the Allied invasion of Sicily was going to be a practice run for D-Day. While obviously on a much smaller scale, it employed comparatively new techniques, combining a large-scale amphibious landing with airborne landings, intended to overwhelm the well-entrenched positions of the Axis forces.

But if Sicily was a practise run, then it left the Allies with a lot of questions to answer before launching the assault on France. Number one: how to launch an airborne landing? The Sicilian trial-run had been a total disaster. Five gliders missed the island completely due to navigation errors, crashing into the sea with the loss of 200 men. And then there was the paratrooper drops. They might as well have not bothered turning up that day: virtually no one landed anywhere near their objective. Scattered randomly through the woods, these soldiers spent the first day of fighting simply trying to find each other. They did not become effective until the men who had landed on the beaches below managed to advance to their hastily improvised positions.

Thankfully, my father was spared this. He was to be part of the second wave, to land on the south east of the island in support of the British Army. His company were to depart for Sicily from the Tunisian port of Sfax, meaning that first they had to be transported across North Africa, from Egypt to Tunisia. It was an unpleasant journey. There were no roads as such, just areas of marginally more compacted sand, meaning progress was slow and backbreakingly uncomfortable. Their convoy had to keep rolling for entire days at a time. The metal body panels on the transporters collected the desert sun, turning the vehicles into huge, mobile ovens, and the canvass roofs that were essential to keep direct sunlight off the troops served also to keep this heat in. The soldiers inside effectively baked in the heat. Dehydration was an issue and several men were sick, meaning that the soldiers were sitting in air thick with the smell of cooked vomit. The relief upon arriving in Sfax, a beautiful city and port, was immeasurable. Recognising that the journey had been deeply unpleasant, the commanders gave the men a day's leave to recuperate.

My father and a couple of the other NCOs took the opportunity to explore the old town. The port had been established by the Romans, and the place was steeped in history, something that always fascinated my father. Together, the men walked beautiful ramparts and shady medieval streets, which were comfortable even in the midday heat. The only thing disturbing this oasis of tranquillity was the stench of the three Polish explorers discovering it. They were still wearing the same uniforms as they had been in that hellish transport.

They were stinking. The locals scurried out of sight when they saw them.

When they came upon a shady square with a fountain at the centre, the sight of the cool, flowing water was like a beacon of relief. The three of them, fully clothed, walked up to its edge, stepped over and lay in the water. The water was warmer than they would have preferred, but nonetheless it was a lot cooler than the air. It felt so refreshing, cooling them and cleaning off the stench, dirt and sweat of their journey. The call to prayer picked up and was echoed by all the other nearby mosques in the city, like an echo rippling through a tunnel. People emerged from all the buildings around the square, and no one even threw the soldiers a glance. They just walked on past, going to immense effort to completely ignore them. Then out of the blue, a little girl came up to the edge of the fountain and without looking up to acknowledge them, placed next to them a basket covered in a cloth, then turned and quickly walked away. My father watched her depart, then leaned over the rim of the fountain's edge. He lifted a corner of the cloth covering and inside the basket were some flat breads, dried figs and currants and a flask of water. It was a simple offering but so touching and generous, as these people clearly did not have much to spare. The cooling water, the beautiful surroundings, the taste of the food and the kindness of the gesture made that moment feel surreal, a rare island of bliss amongst the chaos of war. The three men sat there in the water in silence, soaking it all in.

When it was time to move out, my father and his company assembled with all their equipment and supplies on the harbour side, where a huge destroyer was moored. At one time it had been the pride of the Polish navy, a Wicher-class destroyer called the ORP *Burza*. When Poland fell in 1940, it had been sailed to Britain to avoid it falling into enemy hands. Now here it was, flying both Polish and British flags, ready to transport Polish soldiers to Sicily. The crossing went without incident, the *Burza* making good time, arriving off the southeast coast near Noto, at the beachhead that had been established by the first wave of British and American troops.

For some reason, there is an enduring myth that the invasion of Sicily was something of a walkover – that as soon as the Allies landed, the Italians pretty well immediately capitulated, rolled over and surrendered. That's not quite how it happened. It is true that the beach landings met with less resistance than expected. However, there were two good reasons for that: first of all, British intelligence had employed some subterfuge to fool the Germans into thinking that Sardinia was the intended target, drawing away some of their troops; secondly, most of the military capability on the island was based inland. And there was a fair amount of military capability, including the elite Herman Göring Panzer tank battalions. The principal reason the Allies were able to get a foothold was because of their overwhelming aerial and naval support. When the German tanks moved from their inland bases to the coast, they came into the range of the vast guns of the naval ships moored off the coast. Meanwhile, the RAF, based only 103 miles away in Malta, undertook more than 300 bombing raids on the first day of the invasion alone.

The fiercest fighting took place on the Plain of Catania. Despite its name, much of the terrain was hilly, and the Germans were tightly dug in with heavy guns in all the best defensive positions. It was a very long, slow, drawn out battle, and while in the end the British and their support troops were victorious, it was at the cost of nearly twenty thousand killed or wounded men. Compared to the strategic value of the victory in the grand scheme of things, this was a hugely disproportionate cost. It was also a glimpse of the bigger Italian campaign to come.

After the battle had been won, my father's platoon was ordered to move through the towns and villages situated along a road that ran between Catania and Naxos, on a ridge above the coast in the shadow of Mount Etna. Their mission was to flush out whatever fighting force remained in the area, wherever it may be hidden away. To do so, they had to go door to door, never knowing what they might find on the other side. More often than not they were walking in on families sitting down to dinner, or children playing board games on their living room floor – but you never knew for sure.

The old volcano smoked gently, like a sleeping dragon unwoken by the military mayhem unfolding all around, as the patrols took potshots from German snipers screening the retreating German forces. But the platoon boasted a crack marksman of their own. His nickname was '*Shatan*' – in other words, 'Satan'. Not because of his prowess with a rifle, but because of his recklessness riding a motorcycle. As soon as a report of sniper fire was radioed in, he would ride like the wind to wherever he was needed, roaring up to receive some pointers from the pinned-down patrol. Then he would find his target, neutralise him with one shot, before leaping back onto his motorcycle and roaring back out of town again. Unsurprisingly, he was something of a legend in his brigade.

After the second week of house-to-house searches, it was apparent that the opposition knew they were beaten. As soon as any Italian soldiers were found, they surrendered without hesitation. That took a lot of pressure off my father and the men in his charge. It was part of a general trend in Italy: ordinary Italians were falling out of love with the direction Mussolini was pushing them in. There were demonstrations and riots across mainland Italy. It was becoming clear that they did not share Il Duce's affinity with the Germans.

In one village, my father's patrol was greeted by a man wearing Italian army uniform but with no cap, his tunic unbuttoned and no shirt underneath. A cigarette hung casually from the corner of his mouth. He shouted, '*Venite! Venite!*' and led them with a relaxed swagger to a bunker full of German soldiers who were guarding the road into the village. He even showed the best route to approach the encampment without being spotted by those inside. The Italians were meant to be on the same side as the Germans! My father sent three men down one side of the bunker while he and two others approached from the opposite side and took up positions. Meanwhile, another two took the path the Italian deserter had shown them, which led to the back door. They walked right up to it, posted a grenade, then took cover. After the explosion, the men closed in on the bunker and fired into it. The men at the rear then opened the door and inside found six dead German soldiers with their weapons, a heavy machine gun, and enough ammunition and supplies to hold out for about a week. The Italian soldier peered in behind them and gave them all a round of applause, shouting, '*Bravo! Bravo!*'

My father's experience was far from unique. The Sicilians saw themselves as having close ties with the American forces: it seemed that pretty well everyone on the island of Sicily had family in the States, and a lot of American GIs were of Italian descent too. There were reports that in some areas the local Italian soldiers actually helped the American army land. It is even claimed that the Mafia got involved with supporting the Allies oust the Germans from the island.

Towards the end of his tour in Sicily, something terrible happened to my father. It had a profound effect on him, although it wasn't something he ever really talked about. From what I can gather, he and the other men in his platoon had returned to camp with a handful of Italian prisoners. It had been a pretty slow day; no one had even fired off a single shot. The men were relaxed as they ambled back into camp, laughing and joking with one another, when they heard an explosion from within.

Everyone's initial thought was that the camp was taking mortar fire, and they ran for cover. But after a few moments, it became clear that the explosion was an isolated one. Then they could hear the panicked shouting of men coming from the direction of the explosion. They all ran in the direction of the noise, and within seconds they were on the scene. A Polish soldier had been refuelling his jeep when a spark from his cigarette had ignited the petrol fumes from his jerry can. The force of the explosion had quite literally blown both his arms off, and released a fire ball which had engulfed him totally. His body was burning ferociously. As my father and his men rounded the corner, he was a ball of flames lying on the floor. He appeared to sit up momentarily before falling over sideways to the ground.

That man had been one of my father's closest friends, another corporal from his own platoon and one of the three intrepid explorers who only a few weeks earlier had shared that peaceful moment with him, sitting in a fountain eating figs. Now his head and torso were charred and black, and all anyone could do was try and douse the flames with water and dampened blankets. But it was clear that this man's life was over, not in some heroic deed in battle, but from something as mundane as fuelling a vehicle without thinking to extinguish his cigarette.

Many people remarked that my father had returned home from the Spanish Civil War a very changed man. And in the years that followed the evacuation of Dunkirk, people close to him observed that he was prone to mood swings. But I think that it's fair to say that, after this particular incident on Sicily, his mental health really nose-dived. He became far darker. His jocular nature, once his trademark, all but vanished. Now the only thing that ever seemed to amuse him were cruel practical jokes, usually resulting in the butt of the joke being hurt in some way. The military were not very good at identifying or dealing with mental health issues back then. If you completely lost your senses and could no longer function as a human being, then you would be described as 'shell shocked' and sent home. Anything less dramatic and you just needed to 'cheer up' or 'pull yourself together'. It was war. There was violence and death around every corner. Everyone was sad or frightened. So how was anyone going to notice someone having a breakdown?

After six weeks of fighting, the Italian commander in charge had surrendered and Sicily had officially been captured by the Allies. The biggest problem the Allied commanders now faced was what to do with all their prisoners of war. They had taken over a hundred and twenty thousand German and Italian prisoners, and dealing with them was a logistical nightmare. My father was briefly assigned guard responsibilities for a camp of Italian prisoners of war, but the political fallout from the loss of Sicily made that necessity short-lived. In short order, the Italians rose up against Mussolini and surrendered to the Allies, taking Italy out of their alliance with the Germans within six weeks of the Allied campaign against them. Hitler was so furious that he cancelled a planned attack of Kursk in Soviet Russia to divert troops from the Eastern Front and redeploy them in Italy. Churchill must have been rubbing his hands with glee.

The Allies landed in mainland Italy on 8th September 1943, the same day the new Italian government signed their peace agreement with the Allies, effectively changing sides. My father, Pawel and Henrick landed in Taranto, which had been won by the British a few weeks earlier. By the time they arrived the area was already secured, but even when the British had first arrived, barely a shot had been fired. Pawel and my father were not aware of their proximity to each other. It was only when talking long afterwards that they realised that they had only missed each other by a couple of days. Pawel even swore that he had seen the ***Burza***, my father's ship, sailing towards Italy from the port he and his company were stationed at.

My father's company was given the mission to relieve the British troops that had secured the airfield at Foggia, about one hundred and twenty-five miles north. To get there, they had to move north through a remarkably beautiful natural plateau called the Alta Murgia, which is these days a national park. Sitting in the back of a jeep my father enjoyed the stunning surroundings, historic buildings and forts. He was in his element. Southern Italy in September, compared to the deserts of North Africa and Sicily at the height of summer, was so clement; for the first time in two years, the men could enjoy a hospitable climate. It was a well-earned respite: another one of those seminal moments of peace amidst the hardships of war.

The men would occasionally pull in for refreshments and to stretch their legs at the villages they passed through. Wherever the convoy stopped, they would be greeted with handshakes, pats on the back, carafes of local wine and the most incredible bread, which the area is famous for. It came in odd shapes, sometimes like a fist, sometimes like a bell and sometimes more pebble-shaped like a

French boule. It also had a blackened, brittle crust and tightly compacted flesh with tiny air bubbles. Accompanied by a glass of full bodied local red wine and a morsel of the region's white, crumbly cheese, it was without doubt the most beautiful thing my father had ever tasted.

The journey through the Alta Murgia only took a few days, although the way my father used to talk about it, I think he wished it had gone on forever. You never know where you will discover your own personal heaven. It is rarely in places you expect it to be, and I believe that my father found it there.

Germany was now reduced on both the Western and the Eastern Fronts. However, as much as they may have been weakened, they were still capable of putting up one hell of a fight. And the landscape of Italy itself was going to be a far better ally than the Italian military could ever have been.

The country, as many invading armies have discovered over history, is like a natural fortress, the unforgiving Apennine mountains running like a spine through the middle of the country, with high peaks and craggy outcrops, and between each peak a deep and dangerous river.

When my father's company reached their destination, the provincial capital of Foggia, the true cost of the Italian campaign became clear. The Germans had mounted a gutsy defence of the city and airport, one that had lasted nearly a month. Land assaults had been beaten back, with the Germans well-fortified at all the vantage points. The only way they could be broken, much like in Sicily, was with a relentless battery from the skies. With wave after wave of bombing sorties, the Malta-based RAF and the American bombers now based in Sicily pretty much flattened the entire city. My father and his men were part of the detachment sent to patrol and guard the airbase as it filled up with those same American Flying Fortress bombers. On arrival, they mounted a patrol that saw them trudging through the rubble of the destroyed city. It reminded my father of the sorry state of Madrid when he had been there a few years earlier. There were some giveaway signs of how beautiful the once great and historic city had so recently been; the white walls of the cathedral, though riddled with shrapnel damage and blackened from the smoke of the buildings burned to the ground around it, still stood to an extent. But everything else was just dust and stones. It was a destitute sight.

My father's stationing at Foggia was to last until just after Christmas. His next posting was to be a momentous one. It would prove the Poles' single biggest contribution to the Second World War, and it was where he, Pawel and Henrick were to be reunited. But it is also a place associated with catastrophic casualty rates and poor leadership: the ancient monastery at Montecasino.

Between a Beached Whale and Neptune

Neither my father nor Pawel had been in the front line of a full tilt battle for just about a year. The last time they had seen action, they had been in a desert, and in this wide open, relatively flat and dry terrain, tanks had afforded them a degree of protection. Everything was going to be different at Monte Cassino. It always looked like it was destined to be a German victory, right from the start. The odds of the Allies taking it must have been close to zero.

The Germans had consolidated their positions on what became known as the Gustav Line, and the central point was Monte Cassino. Even while the battle of Sicily was still being fought, more than six months previously, the Germans had identified this as the point they would halt the Allied advance north out of Puglia in mainland Italy. The Line was a network of defences which spanned the entire width of Italy from east to west, just north of the Gagliano river. It consisted of trenches, minefields, gun batteries, bunkers, machine gun nests, and miles and miles of barbed wire all dotted across the most advantageous high points and defensive positions, in an area which was naturally conducive for defending.

The Germans had made the most of every advantage the landscape afforded them, employing the most powerful weaponry available, including the incredible Krupp K5 train-mounted gun, which fired twenty-eight centimetre shells and had a range of fifty miles.

Monte Cassino was roughly halfway between Foggia (where my father had been stationed) and Rome. It stood on a high hilltop on the other side of the appropriately named Rapido River, a perpetual torrent. The monastery was one of the most formidable, impenetrable defensive positions in Italy, famous for having withstood many sieges and battles since being built in the sixth century. With commanding views across the surrounding countryside, whoever occupied Monte Cassino could see everything that was going on in the valleys below for miles around. And as if all that were not enough, when the Germans had retreated from southern Italy, they had devastated all routes north by ploughing up railway lines, blowing up bridges and booby-trapping roads. Getting troops, equipment and supplies up to Monte Cassino was now nearly impossible. Engineers had to spend weeks at a time trying to make a safe route north. Also, the whole region was now in the grips of a very severe winter, and all the approach roads had turned to mud. By the time the soldiers even reached the offensive, they were already cold, tired and soaked to the skin.

How could an assault on Monte Cassino possibly end well? Two previous attempts at taking it by the New Zealanders and the British had failed dismally, providing a taste of things to come. I think if I'd been in command I would have been tempted to say, 'You know what? Let's just leave this one. I've got a bad feeling about it.' That probably would have been quite a good call, as the eventual battle of Monte Cassino was a catalogue of cock ups.

The first cock up was that, a short time before, the monastery had not actually been a German stronghold at all. Upon first occupying the area, the Germans had considered Monte Cassino as a base of operations for all the obvious tactical reasons I have already mentioned. However, their commander had an appreciation for antiquities and concluded against it. It was, after all, a sixth-century monastery of global architectural and spiritual importance; they did not want to risk damaging it by incorporating it into their defences.

The Allies were not so sensitive. Once they had decided it was a German stronghold, they sent a fleet of Flying Fortresses on a bombing raid from Foggia. The relentless firepower of these modern war machines meant that the monastery was completely flattened and lost forever. Naturally enough, the Germans concluded that if the monastery had already been destroyed, they might as well take advantage of its tactical defensive position. What is more, the bombed out remains of the monastery provided far batter cover for heavy artillery guns than the intact buildings could ever have done. The Allies had not only destroyed a sixth-century monastery, they had also created an impregnable twentieth-century fortress. The already imposing Gustav Line was now even more formidable.

This same American-led bombing raid had also inadvertently destroyed the headquarters of the British Eighth Army. Like I said: a catalogue of cock ups.

Another cock up squandered an opportunity to avoid the battle completely. American forces had planned an amphibious landing north of the Gustav line, on the western coast just a few miles south of Rome at Anzio. The Germans had suspected that the Allies might try something like that, especially as their amphibious landings had already worked so well for them in Sicily and southern mainland Italy. However, they could not defend the entire coastline at once, so they took a punt that the landings would happen much further north. This was a stroke of luck for the Allies. When the Americans came ashore at Anzio, they landed unopposed.

Now the smart thing to have done, given that the centre of Rome is only thirty-five miles from Anzio, would have been to take advantage of the element of surprise and advance directly to Rome, while the Germans were caught napping. Take the city, take control until later in the year, cutting off the Gustav Line entirely. It would be a lot easier to smash the the Line after it had been isolated from all sides, starved of resupply and reinforcement, to say nothing of waiting until after the winter had passed.

But that is not what happened. Rather than advance on Rome, the American general at Anzio sat tight on his beachhead and waited. This gave the Germans time to send reinforcements into the area to launch a counterattack. And they sent thousands. They even brought in trainloads of tanks, guns and soldiers from the Eastern Front to do it. They threw everything they had into pushing the Americans back into the sea.

For our part, back home in Les Baudrats, we could not help but notice that the German soldiers stationed around Montceau were looking less soldier-like than they once had. They were mostly now old men in uniform or, at the other end of the scale, new recruits barely old enough to shave. We did not know it at the time, but all the professional soldiers had been moved out of the area to help in the counterattack at Anzio. I remember my aunty Anetka complaining that all the good men had gone from both sides. She had a very unique perspective on the war!

The net result of this hesitation at Anzio meant that the liberation of Rome would drag out for another five months. There was a much more tangible cost, however: the human cost. Over forty thousand were wounded or dead on both sides of the Anzio counterattack, and another fifty-five thousand on the Allied side at Monte Cassino, where the Germans also suffered losses in the tens of thousands. There were also over two thousand civilians caught in the crossfire and killed at Monte Cassino as well. Such staggering numbers are perhaps not surprising when you consider that, from end to end, the battlefield was more than twenty miles long. It took a four-month long battle to finally subdue the Germans and break through the Line to support the stalemate at Anzio. And all of that carnage could so easily have been avoided. The troops were furious about it, as was Churchill back in London, remarking, 'I thought we had sent a wildcat to Italy, but it turns out all we got was a beached whale.'

At the time, probably the only people happy about the battle of Monte Cassino were us in Les Baudrats. For the first time in the war, BBC radio news was reporting stories about a Polish-led battle. Night after night we were told of Polish advances, Polish gains, and in the end, most importantly, in May 1944, Polish victory over the Germans.

We were even told that the Poles were the first to enter the abbey, where they had raised the Polish national flag. We all cheered at hearing that. Michiek got so emotional he started to cry. The pride was palpable, especially knowing that Pawel and my father were there doing their bit. We had no idea at the time that the battle had been so horrific for all involved, not to mention that it could so easily have been avoided. For us it was a rare moment of national pride. After that, when my friends and I played war, it was always as the Polish versus the Germans, rather than the French.

In the war so far, the Poles had been more noted for acts of gallantry that had not really achieved anything, like charging German tanks on horseback. For them to be associated with a victory, especially one won against all the odds, was a new thing. Even King George VI of England flew out to Italy to meet them. A special commemorative medal had been issued to mark the victory and the king was there to oversee the award ceremony.

Both Pawel and my father had played significant roles. Pawel had been one of the very first Allied soldiers to enter the abbey. His platoon had literally fired the first shots inside the building itself. He not only received his battle medal but the George Cross for gallantry. My father, for his part in the battle, was given the honour of being part of the king's cortège. I say 'honour' – I am sure it would have been for most, but for a committed communist it was not exactly the high point it was supposed to be. However, he had to acknowledge that it was nice to get some recognition for a change. And after spending four months lying in mud, a bit of pomp and ceremony was some light relief.

Pawel met up with my father after the ceremony, and they went off to enjoy a drink together with Henrick. Pawel could not help noticing the change in his old friend. The old Stefan would have been so flamboyant in telling the tale of his role in battle. But this Stefan was subdued and withdrawn, a shadow of his former self. The evening after the award ceremony, everyone was given leave. For Henrick and Pawel, this meant a drink-fuelled evening of hilarity and conversation and a general escape from the dirges of war. The evening came to a head, however, when, after a few drinks, Stefan told the story of his friend who had been blown up in Sicily. The tale ended up in an uncontrollable fit of wailing and sobbing, conversation stopped dead in its tracks. Pawel embraced his old comrade and held him tight, Henrick just looked away awkwardly and after about thirty minutes shuffled away into the night. As for Pawel and my father, there they sat for the rest of the evening, my father crying into Pawel's shoulder until the sun rose.

The next day, everyone just had to get on with the war. My father, somewhat embarrassed by his emotional outpouring, gathered his things together, embraced a very concerned Pawel, and headed off to report for duty. He and many of the Free Poles attached to the British Army were put onboard ships and sent back to England. They did not realise it at the time, but a major strategic plan was in place, and they were needed to make up numbers. Pawel and most of the Carpathian Poles remained in Italy to push on.

By June, Pawel and the Allies were in Rome. Once Anzio had been lost, the retreating Germans decided to leave Rome wide open and instead regroup further north. So even though Pawel and Henrick were part of the first wave of the attack, when they entered the city, there were no Germans left to defend it. They literally just marched straight in.

But if, with Rome lost, the Allies expected the German defence of Italy to topple like dominoes, this was wishful thinking. It was still going to be the best part of another year before the Allies got as far as Bologna.

There was another distraction for the Poles in the summer of 1944, one that set blood boiling and pulses racing. As ever, it was reported to the troops in England and Italy around the same time we heard about it from the BBC on our wireless in Les Baudrats. The Russians had been making huge gains against the Germans on the Eastern Front. They had pushed them back across Poland and were now only a few days away from entering Warsaw. We were over the moon. Finally, after five years of occupation, it looked like Poland was about to be a free nation once more. Except it wasn't. This was going to prove yet another example of the Soviets shafting the Poles and the other Allies doing nothing about it.

On hearing that the Soviets were at the gates of Warsaw, the Polish commanders in London gave orders to the resistance in the city to start a revolt, with the streets and squares as a battleground. The plan was to weaken the German grip on the city so that, when the Soviets entered it, Warsaw would already be won. At first, this uprising looked like another example of Polish gallantry, hot on the heels of the victory at Monte Cassino. However, the days passed, turned into weeks then months, and the Soviets did not move any closer to Warsaw to support them. It became clear that the Warsaw resistance were in fact trapped in the city. Access to food, weapons, ammunition and other supplies were squeezed from the west by the Nazis and from the east by the Russians. Sykorsky pleaded with Churchill to release Polish troops from England and Italy and redeploy them in Warsaw so they could liberate their own capital city. Churchill refused, but as a compromise proposed that Polish airmen based at RAF stations around England fly out and drop supplies into the city to support the rebellion. Stalin refused the request. Only a token number of missions were ever allowed. Stalin clearly had a strategy. He wanted the resistance in Warsaw wiped out by the Nazis to save him a job of doing it later himself. After six months, the Russians finally advanced on the city. As the Germans retreated, the Nazi commander gave the order to leave no buildings standing, a command that was carried out with ruthless efficiency. When Stalin's troops eventually did enter Warsaw, in January 1945, they entered it as invaders not liberators, and took control of not so much a capital city as a wasteland.

The Poles had seen it coming. I remember hearing my uncle Michiek discussing it with some friends who visited him at our house.

'They are just betraying us,' he said. 'It's the Katyn massacre all over again. And Churchill is too afraid that Stalin will pack his bags and turn back to Moscow instead of killing more Germans. He will not do anything to rock the boat.' Everyone felt so deflated after the elation of victory at Monte Cassino. It was as if we just didn't matter to anyone. The Poles were to the Allies what Nicole was to my classmates at school.

This 'liberation' of Warsaw sealed the fate of Poland for the next fifty years. But in the more immediate future, it also meant that the Germans on the Eastern Front were now very much on the retreat. By March, the Soviets had entered Vienna, meaning that the Germans to the east had now been pushed all the way back to Germany. The Italian campaign finally came to a head with the liberation of Bologna in April, putting another big dent in German morale.

When my father had been shipped out of Italy earlier in the year, he had been taken to Portsmouth and then billeted in a camp somewhere on the edge of the New Forest. Last time he had been in the UK, in the year or so before he had been sent to Africa, it had been a relatively cushy posting. This time things were a bit different. The training schedule was relentless, and the training itself a lot more rigorous. The troops knew that they were training for a large-scale amphibious landing in northern France, but they did not know exactly where or when it would happen. Not too far from the camp was a tributary of the Solent, and day after day they would practise sailing around the cove and landing on the beach there. Landing craft were awful things. They had high sides so you could not see out, and flat bottoms so you could feel every single wave and bump against the bottom of the boat. If you were prone to sea sickness, travelling any distance in a landing craft was sure to make you suffer. And the English Channel is quite bumpy enough to guarantee this every time my father and his comrades went in one. And they went in one a lot.

Any sense of relief when you stepped off your landing craft was short-lived. On the beach, the troops would be warned that live ammunition was to be used, to add a bit of urgency to proceedings;

they also had to contend with barbed wire defences and training NCOs with flamethrowers. This went on day in and day out. The invasion had originally been planned for May, but did not actually take place until early June. Throughout April the beach landing training was peppered with embarkation drills, and it was never clear if these were actually drills or the invasion itself. The day would begin with an alarm sounding at around three in the morning. All the men would run out onto parade and stand to attention. In the silence you could hear the sounds of transports from other nearby camps thundering along the main road in convoy. Then the order would be given to gather all your equipment and belongings and climb onboard a waiting lorry. Off they would all trundle, to the camp gates and then out on to the road, already thick with traffic, all heading towards the port.

The scale of the planned invasion was nowhere more clear than the port. There would be literally thousands of troops marching on to ships, whilst tanks, big guns, shells, vehicles and supplies were loaded on with cranes and winches. As they approached the gangplank onto their ship, every man would be handed rations and ammunition then sent on their way. My father had butterflies in his stomach every time; every time it felt real, the morning of the big one – whatever the big one was to be. Then after a few hours of this mayhem, an officer would announce that it was all a drill and everybody had to stand down and wait for their turn to march back down the gang-plank, give back their rations and ammunition and return to camp. The drills were huge operations in and of themselves, and no doubt similar drills were taking place at all the other ports along the south coast. By the time D-Day itself came around, the troops had already practised every element of it many times over.

When the day came, the only thing different was that, once everyone was on board, no one came forward to say it was a drill. The ships cast off with the tide and set sail out into the English Channel. And what a sight they were. The sea was so full of ships it looked like you could have walked across the channel using them as steppingstones. It was truly incredible to see.

My father's unit had by now been absorbed into the British Fiftieth Infantry Division, and soon they neared a small coastal village called Le Hamel. It was part of the beach codenamed 'Gold', and their objective was to secure it and move west along the coast to meet up with the Americans who had landed at 'Omaha'. There they would secure the coastal town of Arromanches, where the Allies would build their floating 'Mulberry' harbours to establish a supply line.

As my father's ship approached the coast, the ships around them opened fire. The sound of their great guns was deafening. Then their own ship joined in, every *boom* making the whole craft creak and rattle and reel from the force of it. Cargo nets were thrown down either side of the ship, and a flotilla of landing craft, like a fleet of taxis, made their way alongside. As soon as the landing craft were in place, the men were ordered in waves to clamber down the nets and load them up. The rocking motion of the ship, the bouncing of the landing craft, the booming guns, the explosions in the sea around them from German return fire... it is fair to say that the atmosphere was charged. It was also really windy and the sea quite choppy. Men kept getting tangled up in the nets as they clambered down into the landing craft, so my father was stationed halfway down the net, hanging on by his arms and legs, to untangle people as they got caught up.

Once their ship was all but empty, he clambered down the net himself with his commanding officer and some other officers. They were to ride in on the last landing craft. Even though my father had managed to avoid being seasick in all the beach landing practice runs, on this day nerves got the better of him. He did not like to show weakness, especially to his superiors, so he was absolutely mortified. In the great scheme of things, I am sure they all had other things on their minds. To him, though, the incident overshadowed every other memory he had of one of the most momentous days in history.

Even though he was one of the last off his own ship, my father was still part of the first wave of attack. He was on the beach by 9am, less than two hours after the first man. Arriving on the beach at the same time as his commander, he at least had a very clear idea of his objective; the downside was that he had no idea where his platoon was. He was quickly assigned to another platoon, under the command of another officer he had landed with.

Most of the initial resistance met by the men was from German infantry, a like-for-like exchange of small arms fire. The Allies inevitably won the contest through superior numbers. However, a huge German gun battery, not far away at Longues-sur-Mer, frustrated Allied attempts to land further troops. While three out of four guns had been disabled, one had been salvageable, and the defending Germans managed to get it back into operation by the afternoon. It was not so much a concern for the men on the beach, but to those troops landing to reinforce them.

The biggest problem my father faced was that the Germans had fortified the houses along the beachfront. Each one was like a mini castle, and it was back to fighting from house to house, much like in Madrid and Sicily. My father being an old hand at this, his platoon punched well above their weight compared to other units, despite the fact he did not know any of the people he was fighting with. At the end of the first day, they had managed to clear a beachhead as far as the big guns at Longues-sur-Mer, and by the following day the garrison stationed there had surrendered. The rest of my father's unit had also succeeded in meeting up with the Americans on the beach below the battery, and securing Arromanches.

The next part of his mission was to move inland to liberate the ancient town of Bayeux; then it would be onto the slow and arduous drive east across France.

By the end of the year, Pawel's company had fought and liberated Breda in the Netherlands and were the heroes of the city. My father and his brigade were heading towards the banks of the river Rhine through Belgium. Germany was now in full retreat. Surely it would not be much longer before the war would be over, and they could return home to see the family, friends and places that they loved and had left behind?

Victory in Europe

It is so often the case that, when you wish passionately and desperately for something momentous to happen, when it does actually come about, it's not all it was cracked up to be. I and everybody I knew had prayed and hoped and dreamed of the day the war would be over. We should have known better. War is such a messy business, where nothing seems to go as you expect it to; even how it ends has the potential to disappoint. Looking at the bigger picture, of course, the German surrender was a brilliant thing. How many lives were saved in that instant? How many soldiers, prisoners, Jews, Gypsies and other people locked up in concentration camps were able to return home to their families? But for people like us, in our household in Les Baudrats, it was not so decisive a moment as I had hoped. I suppose, in my own little mind, I thought the Germans would surrender on the Monday, and by the following Friday my father and my uncle Pawel would be home. We'd all be grateful, have a party, everyone would be happy, and we would all live happily ever after.

No other episode of my life had ever worked out like that, so I'm not sure why I thought this would be any different. I suppose it must have been to do with the fact that everything that gave me pain seemed in some way down to the war. 'Where's your father?' Fighting in the war. 'Why is there no food?' Because of the war. 'Can I play with Klaus?' No, his parents are German... And so it went on. As simplistic as it was, I genuinely thought that if you removed the war, then no more pain.

Not the case.

The first die had been cast a few months before the war ended, when my great grandfather had died. He had lived to a really good age, but the sadness of his passing tinged everything that followed. No matter how good the news, our first thoughts would be, 'If only Josef were here. He would have enjoyed this.'

For us in the Montceau-les-Mines area, the war was over when we were liberated on 6th September 1944. There was no Battle of Montceau as such. Somehow, everyone knew that the Americans were on their way, and then one morning the Germans just seemed to disappear into thin air. No one saw them leave or heard the vehicles go; when we woke up, they just weren't there anymore.

Word spread not just in Montceau but every village for miles around. In our house, we had all planned to catch the bus into town together, but my mother and Aunty Anetka were up to their usual faffing around with hair curlers, makeup and dress choices, so we missed the bus, and the rest of the household went into town without us. Fortunately, my granny had spotted my uncle Jakub and aunty Mira on the already crowded streets of Montceau. She dispatched him and his tiny little car back to the house to collect us. So there we were, in all our Sunday best, being driven into town to join the excited throng pouring into the centre of town. We found the rest of the family and pushed into the crowd to stand with them. There wasn't much actually happening, but nonetheless the excited anticipation grew. Everyone, from young children to people in their eighties, were standing at the roadside in a state of manic expectation, waiting to see what would happen.

Then the cheers started. We all started cheering too, not put off at all by the fact that we could not see anything worth cheering about. Then three American jeeps with American servicemen on board thundered through the town at breakneck speed. The soldiers looked jolly enough and waved, but they passed in a matter of seconds, and the cheering was over. Everyone just looked at one another.

Was that it?

None of us had ever been to a liberation before, so we were not sure what to expect. But I think we had all been anticipating a bit more of a drawn-out affair than that. Another half an hour went by, and another wave of cheering spread through the crowd as an American motorbike and a couple of jeeps thundered through at the same pace as the first one.

Finally, after a good hour or two, a slightly more sustained cheer rose up. This time, however, many craned their necks to see what was going on before committing to the cheer themselves. They needn't have worried. This time it was a proper parade. An endless file of American soldiers came into view, marching down the street, flanking transported trucks on either side. The crowd were ecstatic, cheering, laughing, dancing, shouting... The GIs marched through the streets beaming from ear to ear. They threw sweets into the crowds for the children, and I was absolutely ecstatic when one of them winked at me and threw over a bar of chocolate. I had never tasted chocolate in my life. My head was about to pop as it flew through the air towards me, and in the peak of emotion, I missed the catch and the chocolate bar fell to the ground. I darted for it, but before I could reach it, a scrawny man standing behind me put his foot over it to stop me. He gave a smug, victorious sneer, and my big doe eyes started to fill up, his outline blurring as huge tears welled up in my eyes. The grin on his face changed to a look of terror at the thought that I was about to scream the place down, and he quickly lifted his foot off it, bent down and thrust it into my hands. 'Here you are, little girl,' he said. 'I was only joking. It's for you.' I snatched it from him, reluctantly saying thank you, but the look on my face told him what I was really thinking. Only joking my foot! He'd had every intention of stealing my chocolate!

I clutched it tight. I felt so proud and somehow managed to restrain myself from eating it until we got home. Oh my God, it tasted amazing! I have never had an experience in my life as good as the first time I ever tasted chocolate. I wasn't sure if I was going to like it at first, but everyone had so built up how lucky I was to have it, I felt duty bound to at least pretend, even if it tasted awful. I tried to make the first taste really last, only breaking off a tiny piece from the corner. But once the thick, sweet, gooey morsel started to melt on my tongue, it was like I had been possessed. I could not gobble up the rest of it fast enough. At least, when it was all gone, I could still feel the last remnants sticking to the inside of my cheeks. I ran my tongue along them to soak up every last bit. The family were all watching me, and they laughed out loud. I had a smile a mile wide, which I could not have shaken off if I'd tried. My uncle Michiek gave me a pat on the head. So far, the war ending was going really well for me.

But things took on a totally different tone the following morning.

Michiek and Nadia had both gone off to their respective places of work early that day, and my grandfather Zarec was out digging in the back garden. Aunty Anetka was in her bedroom getting ready for the day, while my granny and my mother and I were sitting down to breakfast. Like most breakfasts this had been pretty uneventful, but just as I was taking a bite of a crust of bread, I heard something of a commotion out in the street. There seemed to be a lot of very animated people gathering outside our house. Then there came a pounding on our door. It made me jump. My granny went to open the door, but before she could, it burst open. Through the open door I could see a jeering, angry mob outside our house. Two women and three men were suddenly standing in our kitchen. One of them was the podgy local butcher, another was his wife, there was a woman from two streets over, and the rest were all people I recognised from church and round and about. They were all yelling at the top of their voices at my granny. They shouted so loudly that it was difficult to understand what anyone was saying.

My grandfather appeared behind them, coming in from the garden to see what all the fuss was about. One of the men, possibly startled by his appearing from behind, turned suddenly and started pushing him in the chest, shouting and gesticulating at him. Even though my grandfather was getting on a bit, this was a red rag to a bull. He took a swing at the intruder, and suddenly the two of them were punching seven bells out of each other. I was a little girl of six watching this unfolding in my kitchen. What the hell was going on? I burst into tears and clung tightly to my mother's dress for dear life.

Some other people came in from the street to try and restrain my grandfather, and with that Anetka emerged. Like a wave, they all surged towards her. They were yelling, 'Collaborator!' and 'Get the collaborator whore!' The butcher, who had previously been more than happy to be intimate with her, reached out and angrily grabbed her by the arm. She instinctively resisted and tried to shake him off. A couple of other people joined in and reached out and grabbed her as well. She tried to fight them off and pull back, but there were too many of them. She started to panic, her shouting descending into tears and manic screaming when, out of the blue, one of the men who had been restraining my grandfather straightened up, bounded across the room and punched her to the floor. My granny, mother and I all gasped a sharp intake of breath, my granny bringing her hand up to cover her mouth. We just could not believe what we were seeing. The mob dragged her screaming out of the house, two holding her arms, and the butcher's wife pulling her by her hair. I will never forget the look in her eyes as she was dragged across the kitchen floor. It was a look of sheer terror. Like a lamb to the slaughter. They dragged her into the street and came to a stop in front of the rest of the crowd. They all jeered, taking turns spitting at her and kicking her on the ground. Then one of them grabbed a fistful of her hair, pulled her up to her feet and frogmarched her down the street. All the while she was screaming for mercy, but the mob were in no mood for mercy.

My granny told my mother to tend to me. She gave my grandfather a handkerchief to stem a nosebleed he had been given, and the two of them then set off down the street at a discreet distance behind the mob. I was inconsolable, scared out of my wits.

Anetka had been rounded up along with any other poor women of the village who had fraternised with German soldiers. The local resistance men (who were now in charge since the Germans had gone) had set up a row of chairs in the square. They stood guard over them, armed with machine guns. The now hysterical girls were pushed forward in front of the chairs and ordered to sit down. The girls were wailing and sobbing and clinging to each other for comfort. Most were bleeding from the rough treatment they had received from the mob. One by one they had all their hair brutally cut off with a pair of sheep shears. The mob standing round them laughed and jeered and spat at them. Humiliation was to be their punishment for their poor judgement in men. It was like something from the Middle Ages.

After a couple of hours, Anetka returned to the house, escorted home by my grandparents. She looked a sorry sight. Her clothes were dirty and torn, her hair had been shorn to the skin save for a few random tufts, and her scalp was bleeding from where the shears had nicked her. She had two black eyes and a cut lip, and her face was tracked with tears. She was still sobbing. My granny took her to her room and put her to bed. She didn't leave the house for weeks after. As cruel as it might be to say, she was always rather vain. She did not have much going for her other than her good looks, which had so callously been taken from her, so now she was in a really sad state.

The other shock I received when our part of the war ended was that my father didn't just suddenly appear a few days later. In fact, it would be another two years before I would see him again, and another three before he became a permanent fixture. Even though we had been liberated in our little corner of France, the war in Europe was far from over. It was to rage on for another eight months. At the time we were liberated, my father was still in Belgium. But we could at least now write to each other. We were no longer under German occupation, so we didn't need to worry about our letters being intercepted and read, with a visit from the Gestapo the next day as a result.

My mum wrote to him, I wrote to him, his sister Anetka wrote to him, and we would occasionally get a letter back – never one each, always one letter addressed to all of us. Pawel and Nadia also wrote to each other. However, she got a letter nearly twice a week. My mother, who had a jealous predisposition, used to get furious every time Nadia got a letter and we didn't. We didn't realise it at the time, but my father was really struggling mentally. Written displays of affection, even feigned interest in what was going on at home were really hard for him. My mother, of course, instinctively dived at the wrong conclusion. She was certain his lack of correspondence was down to his having a string of affairs with everything in a skirt from Marrakech to Berlin. She could never truly let go of this thought. For years and years after the war was over, she would level this accusation at him whenever they argued (which was all the time).

But as much as my father was failing his family, he was excelling as a soldier. He had been promoted to sergeant, was highly decorated and had the respect of everyone he served with. His unit was on the banks of the Rhine by the beginning of March 1945 and were part of the race to take Berlin. Each of the Allied commanders could see that the Germans were in the dying moments of their campaign and that surrender was now inevitable. So the most important thing for each of them now were the bragging rights over who got to enter Berlin first. Vanity is rarely helpful when it comes war. In the east, Stalin was in the best position, and the British and Americans threw everything into catching up with him, with the disastrous Operation Market Garden. When that failed, it was inevitable that a Russian general would be first to enter the city. But still troops on the front line were pushed to catch up. Within a month all three forces were in Berlin. The Russians had got there first, but the city was still not secure, and fighting continued. My father was with one of the first wave of companies from the western side to join in the fight. The troops my father was facing still contained some professional soldiers, but most were a pathetic shadow of the Germans he had been fighting in North Africa and Italy. They were mainly young men who could not tell one end of a rifle from the other, drafted in as a last ditch defence of the Reich. For seasoned soldiers like my father, who had fought their way across Europe since D-Day, they presented nothing more than a paper thin challenge.

The Germans finally surrendered in May, and that meant that the war in Europe was officially over. It was a time for celebration. We had a huge carnival in Montceau. I was part of a troop of Polish children who wore national costume and joined in the procession through the town that day. My family were very proud. Pawel had arrived in Berlin and had met up with my father, but they both remained in Germany for a few more months as part of the peace-keeping force. Back in London the official VE Day celebrations saw a nation united in relief and pride. Allied troops took part in events to mark the occasion all over the country. But not the Poles. For some reason they were not invited to take part in celebrating the end of a war they had fought so hard to help win. This snub has been a source of bitterness amongst Polish service personnel ever since.

After a few months of peacekeeping duties, my father, Pawel, Poles from the Carpathian Brigade and those of the Western Army were shipped back to barracks in Edinburgh – even Vojtek, the bear who had been their mascot since their arrival in North Africa, who was housed in Edinburgh zoo. One of my father's rare letters described in very unemotive language what happened next. The Polish free army was to be disbanded, both the western army under Sykorsky, and the Carpathians, who were technically part of the eastern army under Anders.

Those with Polish citizenship were to return to Poland. Those like my father and Pawel, who were Poles but had French citizenship, were given a choice. They could return to France or, if they wanted, could start a new life in Poland. This was not an option many were interested in, mainly because it was already clear that the Russians had no intention of moving out of Poland now they were there. Memories of what had happened in Katyn Woods were still fresh in everyone's minds. And they were right to be wary. What everyone was unaware of at the time was that Churchill had already done a deal with Stalin a year earlier. He would hand Poland over to the Russians as long as they agreed to let Britain keep her interests in Greece. Poland had been shafted yet again, to the surprise of no one. They were getting used to being shafted by this point.

There was, however, a third option presented to the Polish

soldiers in Edinburgh, and it was made regardless of their country of citizenship. Much as France had suffered a catastrophic loss of workforce during the First World War, so too had Britain during the second. Any serving Poles who had skills high in demand but short in supply (such as miners) were also given the choice to remain in the UK if they wished. They were offered British citizenship for themselves and their immediate families and a guarantee of work in one of the UK's many prosperous coal fields.

For Pawel the choice was a no brainer. His home, his family, his friends, his job, his life were all in France. He desperately wanted to get home to his Nadia and start a family of their own. He had thought of little else throughout the war. Fantasies about him, Nadia and a brace of children with their own little house somewhere on the edge of Sanvignes or St Vallier had kept him going even in the most desperate of situations the war had thrown at him.

For my father, things were not so clear. First of all, I always got the impression that he regretted marrying my mother – that he felt he had been trapped into it. Which to be fair, he had been. Secondly, and this was something I never understood, for some reason he hated living in France. For all the years he had lived there, he had never bothered to even learn the language, not until his time in Spain, when he had found himself in a trench with a bunch of comrades who only spoke French. This anti-French sentiment was not out of loyalty to Poland. As much as he used to grumble about how boring and pedestrian life in Sanvignes and Montceau was compared to Gdansk, he didn't want to live in Poland either. I suppose that when he first arrived in France, he was just a spoiled teenager having a tantrum about moving away. In a few years' time I would totally be able to relate to that sentiment. But he had never quite got past his initial dislike for his adopted country.

Before being shipped out to North Africa, he had spent a year stationed in Scotland, specifically Edinburgh. He loved Edinburgh. It appealed to his taste for historic buildings, and it was a bustling cosmopolitan city where there was a lot going on. In that year he had gone to the trouble of learning some English. He was not in any way fluent in the language, but he could do the basics: greetings, please and thank you, and ordering food or drink in a café or shop. So after he had thought about his choices, he decided he would stay in Britain, and he wrote a letter to tell us.

My mother went through the roof. Both she and Nadia wrote to Pawel asking him to plead with my father to see sense, but my father was having none of it. The more they tried to dissuade him, the more obstinate he became. He applied to remain in the UK and was given a work visa and assigned work in the coal mine at Senghenydd in the South Wales coalfield. He was to leave Edinburgh at once and would be temporarily billeted in an army barracks in Caerphilly until he could find accommodation of his own.

His initial experience of his new life was not too bad. A handful of other Poles had made the same choice as him, and while he had never met any of them before, they had all served together, seeing action in Monte Cassino and Normandy, so there was plenty to talk about. For a while, his new home had all the benefits and comradeship of being in the army, without the sticky issue of people shooting or shouting at you or telling you what to do. I am fairly sure he enjoyed the freedom.

But like all men, these new arrivals had urges. And getting women who speak a different language to you could be problematic. However, they had learned a few tricks while travelling through Europe, which had served them well in overcoming any language barriers. One such trick was to place their penis in the hands of a local girl and burst into tears! Apparently it used to work like a charm in Italy and Holland. So they brought this charming tradition to Wales, and amazingly it had a very good success rate there too. Soon some of the Poles ended up with girlfriends in the town, and this caused friction with local boys, the stereotypical 'coming over here, taking our women and our jobs' brigade. Saturday night fights outside pubs in Caerphilly became regular fixtures, and soon this became a real issue where my father was concerned.

In this era, fighting in pubs on a Saturday night was seen by many of the protagonists as a sport. It was just part of what you did on a night out. My father had boxed for his regiment during the war, so he was clearly quite useful with his fists. But that wasn't the main problem. Once a fight was over, people generally would peel away. Sometimes afterwards they would even make up, congratulate each other on how they had fought and buy each other drinks. My father, though, just didn't know when to stop. He would keep going until his friends had to pull him away. The war took many things from many people. It had stripped my father of any compassion, mercy or basic humanity. Once he was engaged in conflict, in his mind, it was to the death, and in peacetime, you just cannot behave like that. It was clear to his friends that if they didn't do something to dampen his temper, it was only a matter of time before my father did someone some real damage. Or worse.

To deal with him, they would spike his beer with spirits in the early part of any night out, so he would be too drunk to fight later in the evening. As a strategy it worked, but it had the undesirable side effect of making my father realise that the only time he was truly at peace with himself was when he was so drunk he could not think. This unfortunately started his inevitable slide into alcoholism.

After a while he got himself a proper place to live, renting a bed in a room which he shared with another miner. It was in a house in a village called Abertridwr, which was roughly halfway between Caerphilly and Senghenydd. The landlady who ran the place was a very strait-laced Welsh matriarch. She had a stern face and pursed lips, a tightly bound bun of grey hair on top of her head and always wore a tabard. She went to Chapel every Sunday and hosted Bible classes in her parlour on a Wednesday evening. She disapproved passionately of her tenant's drinking, which might at least have slowed down his resolve to drink himself to death.

In Sanvigne, by way of contrast, Pawel had arrived home to rapturous scenes of emotion, relief and pride. We had a big party to celebrate his return. He was everybody's hero, and all his medals were mounted on a board and hung over the fireplace in our house. It was only to be there for a short time, however, as he was determined to make his dreams of starting a family a reality. Within a few months, he and Nadia had got themselves a little cottage in Les Gautherets. As you would expect with Nadia, the challenge of making it her own was a dream come true in itself. I have never known anyone who loved being so frantically busy. The house was always immaculate, the front festooned with so many pots and hanging baskets full of begonias that in the summer you could not see the house for flowers. And every single stone on the gravel paths through the garden seemed to have been scrubbed and placed in a specific order. Inside was the same. The tiled floors and surfaces were scrubbed daily. The whole place was kept cleaner than a science lab. But despite that, it never felt anything other than homely. As obsessive as Nadia might have been about cleanliness and order, the warmth of her soul and her generous nature always somehow shone through.

Within a year, the dream was complete. Nadia was pregnant and she was soon to give birth to a baby boy, Lucasz. As we grew up, though separated by nations, he and I would always remain very close. Coincidentally, Mira also fell pregnant that year; she would have a little girl within a month of Nadia, named Alinka after my grandmother. Suddenly I was not the only one of my generation.

So while life for my father back in Wales was looking very bleak, life for us in France was looking the best it had ever been. There was no doubt in the minds of my aunts, uncles and grandma that something had to be done to try and reconcile the two worlds. To them, my having a father and my mother having a husband were the most important priorities. Any alternative seemed unthinkable. But how were they going to be able to pull this off?

Land of My Father

The last time my mother and I had heard from him, my father had been organising our passage to Wales. He would send for us, he said, when he had found us somewhere suitable to live. But he didn't seem to be in any particular rush. Soon we had been stuck in this limbo for nearly a year, and my mother was at her wit's end. She, Anetka and my granny went to petition Pawel to get involved with moving things on – preferably by persuading my father to drop this whole 'living in Wales' madness and come back to the family in France. Pawel was initially reluctant to get involved. He had already tried to talk him around when they had been in Scotland together, and he knew how obstinate my father was. He was also very wrapped up in making a life for his own family. But a chance correspondence from an old comrade in arms changed his mind.

Out of the blue, Pawel received a letter from someone he had served with, a man called Novak. They had both been corporals in the same regiment during the war. They had seen a lot of action together and, like most of the men Pawel had fought with, had become close friends and kept in touch with occasional letters. A lot of demobbed soldiers had done the same, and between them they formed a network that stretched right across Europe and the USA.

At this particular point in time, the Polish community in South Wales was quite small and consisted pretty well entirely of ex-service personnel, meaning everyone knew everyone else. It included a man called Leon, who had grown up with Novak near Krakow and had served as a sergeant in a Polish cavalry regiment. After the war, Leon had accepted British citizenship and a job at the Marconi factory in Cardiff. He knew my father, who was based no more than a short drive away, and he was aware that they had friends in common. So on this occasion, when Leon wrote to Novak as part of their regular correspondence, he asked him to pass on to Pawel his concerns that my father was becoming a mess. That he was not acclimatising to life in peace time. That he was, in essence, an out of control drunk.

It transpired that my father's drinking had caused him to lose his accommodation in Abertridwr and that he was staying with friends wherever they were able to put him up. Leon went on: 'If this man has a wife and daughter in France, then maybe they are the steadying influence he needs to get himself sorted out and his life back together. But if nothing is done, I fear he is destined for a life in prison or to die in a gutter somewhere.'

These were very hard words to read, and they could not be ignored. Pawel called a meeting, inviting Michiek and my granny to get together at his house (so Anetka, my mother and I would not hear the conversation). Between them they had to decide how to respond. What could they do for the best? Popping over to have a quick word was not an option. Travelling across Europe in the 1940s was not so easy to do, unless you were in an invading army or were very rich. Today, you can travel from Montceau to Cardiff by train, or you can fly from Lyon or Paris in an hour, for a few pounds. Back then, the journey would have taken around three days and would have cost a month's wages.

However, the perfect opportunity to lure my father back to France would soon present itself. Both Nadia and Mira were in the later stages of their pregnancies and were due to give birth within a few weeks of each other. The family could have a joint baptism for both babies and arrange a big family celebration. Once my father was back in the country, reunited with his wife and daughter, he would be reminded how great it was to have family around him and Pawel could work on him to get him to remain in France. The family would agree to rally around and help him get back on his feet with whatever he needed: help getting a job, loans of money, a roof over his head and moral support.

It was quite a good plan, although not exactly foolproof. There was a possibility that he might just ignore the invitation. To try and prevent this, Pawel made direct contact with Leon in Cardiff, winning himself an ally close to my father's ear who could persuade him to come to the baptism if he had any doubts.

The other possibility was that he could turn up to the baptism, get blind drunk, cause a scene and end up getting disowned by everyone. Just as bad, he could come to the baptism, get reminded how much he did not want to be with my mother, and run a mile.

No one consulted me in any of this. With the benefit of hindsight, I would honestly say that any one of these 'disastrous' outcomes would have been better than what actually happened. There is no doubt that my childhood during the war had been traumatic. I had contended with food shortages, my mother's abuse, diphtheria, nearly drowning, school friends getting killed, general restrictions on my liberty, and – horror of horrors – a distinct lack of new toys. But now that the war was over, most of that had changed. I loved my uncle Pawel, who had left for the war when I had been just a little girl; there was now plenty of room at our house, with Mira and Nadia having moved out and my great uncle passing; there was the excitement of having two new babies on the way; and I could play with whomever I liked whenever I liked. My mother was still occasionally horrible to me, but she had at least mellowed, from time to time even getting a bit maternal, and anyway, I was surrounded by such a big family, I did not have to rely solely on her for affection. The last thing in the world I wanted to do now was to move away and leave all this behind. Unlike my father, I adored France: the people, the countryside, the food, the music, the culture, the language, the literature, the history, the climate… And even though where we lived was industrialised and very diluted with Polishness, you were never far away from all the 'real' France that I loved.

As predicted, Lukasz and Alinka were born within three weeks of each other. Everybody in our family was absolutely overjoyed. It was like a marker that the rubbish times were over, and the good times beginning. Nadia hatched up plans for the joint baptism and celebration and went about organising them with her usual degree of fervour. Part of the preparations was the task of getting a letter of invitation out to my father via Leon.

For my own part, I was really looking forward to my father coming over. I had been told how much he loved me and how he used to play with me as a baby, and it had been heavily hinted that he might be staying in France after the baptism. That to me sounded like a positive thing. Back then, it was seen as a tragedy that a little girl might grow up without both her parents.

When the invitation got to him, my father was pretty much at rock bottom. He had already lost his own accommodation, and then had been chucked out by the first friend he had moved in with, and things were not going well with the second. To cap it all, he was in danger of losing his job too, if he didn't buck up his ideas and stay off the drink.

He was not a man who could admit to failure easily, so when he read the invitation, he had no intention whatsoever of attending. The last thing he wanted was to see the whole family happy and settled in France while he was a wreck in self-imposed exile. Especially when everyone had warned him against it. He believed that going back to Montceau for a family celebration would amount to a week of hearing, 'I told you so,' from everyone. Not to mention having to kowtow to my mother. The plan to repatriate him seemed doomed to failure before it had even begun.

I had never wanted to leave France, and with my father's rejection of the invite, I had no idea how close I came to getting my own way. Fate, however, had a card up her sleeve, which she played with immaculate timing.

The pit my father was working in, Senghenydd, was synonymous with disaster. An explosion underground had claimed the lives of over 400 miners at the beginning of the twentieth century. Despite that, due to the massive demand for coal, the pit was still in operation. And while nothing on that scale ever happened there again, mining was still a very dangerous occupation, and there were frequent accidents. The South Wales coalfield was well known for having a really shallow coal seam. Miners frequently had to work on their backs or bellies, just to have access to the coalface. And it was in just such an environment that, one shift, a large section of rock came loose above where two of my father's colleagues were working, only a matter of inches away from him.

The weight of the fall crushed the two of them and they were both killed instantly. It also cut my father off from any escape route, and blocked out all the lighting. You don't know what darkness truly looks like unless you have been in a pit with the lights off. Even on the darkest nights, there is always some light source somewhere. Three miles underground, there is none. With no light, no sound and unable to move due to the rockfall, for a while my father could not be sure if he was not dead himself. He tried to reconnect the light on his helmet to his battery pack but could not get it to work. Eventually he was able to strike a match. There was no question of getting his bearings; he could not see far enough to make any difference. He was lying on his back with no more than a foot or two of space above him. He knew he needed to conserve what little air he had, so he had to resign himself to lying there, with all his senses numbed, in the hope that there would be a rescue. Fortunately for him, while he had been cut off by the rockfall that had killed his two colleagues, the rest of his shift had a clear escape route and could raise the alarm.

When the rescue party came, they worked through the area of collapsed rock and coal and moved out the mangled corpses of the two unlucky ones who had been crushed. They then reached the small recess beyond where my father had been trapped. He could hear them chipping away and started calling out. They paused their chipping for a second, listening out. He called again. This time they had definitely heard him. He could hear them going at it with more vigour. Then a shaft of light shone in and a voice said in a thick Welsh accent, 'You fuckin' lucky bastard.'

Even though he told his rescuers he thought he could walk, they carried him out on a stretcher and put him in an ambulance. They checked him over at the hospital, and amazingly, he appeared to have only a few superficial injuries, just cuts and bruises, although they kept him in overnight just to be on the safe side. He was back in work after a few days, and to his surprise found that he was now famous. He had gone from being 'that fuckin' Polish bloke' who no one spoke to, to 'that fuckin' lucky Polish bloke' who everyone regarded as a form of celebrity – especially when they found out about his war record. This did a lot to lift his self-esteem, something in which he had been sorely lacking since being de-mobbed from the army.

A week or so later the funeral of the two men was held, and my father went along to pay his respects. He was so moved by the singing in the chapel that, I think it is fair to say, it changed his life. He was, after all, a musician himself. He had never heard anything like the sound of a Welsh chapel so full of miners that there was standing room only. They were all singing on top of their voices, every single voice with perfect tone and pitch. Welsh hymns like 'Aberystwyth' and 'Llef' were belted out at full tilt with four-part harmonies. It was an awesome sound, enough to make the hairs on the back of anyone's neck stand up, and given my father's fragile state of mind, it made him weep like a baby. There was no shame in weeping; he was at a funeral, and it made him look more human, more in touch with the community and his work colleagues, more like 'one of the boys'. It earned him a lot of respect.

After that people would go out of their way to talk to him and help him out. A colleague he had barely spoken to in all the time he had been in the pit came over one morning saying, 'I heard you're looking for a place to live? If you're interested, me and the wife have got a spare room we rent out to lodgers. It's empty now and it's yours if you're interested.' My father took him up on the offer and, as this man was also the choirmaster of the colliery male voice choir, he decided to join the choir as well. His pronunciation of Welsh words was pretty suspect, but he could read music, hold a note and harmonise, so he was welcomed with open arms.

Another epiphany struck my father at the funeral, as the bodies were being interred to their graves. One of the men had had a wife and young daughter. When my father saw their outpouring of grief, it got him thinking about his responsibilities. Now I'm not saying this event cured him overnight. That he went to this funeral an alcoholic and left a pillar of society. Mentally he was still messed up. And he was still drinking. However, it caused a big enough change in him to make him realise that he had a good life to live if only he chose to embrace it; big enough to convince him to come to the baptism in France after all.

I was so delighted to see him. I had still been quite tiny when he'd left for the war, so at first I didn't recognise him. And likewise he could not get over the fact that I was now a girl, not a baby. He embraced me for what seemed like an uncomfortably long time. But his reunion with my mother was not such a happy one. When she saw him, she stood in the doorway with a face like thunder and her arms folded. She silently swung out a cheek to be kissed, then, once he had given her a peck, turned on her heels and walked away. She kept this up for the whole of his first day, until in the end Pawel and my granny had to take her to one side and have a word with her. The plan was to get the two of them back together, and her shunning my father at every opportunity really was not helping.

The baptism went well, and the party afterwards was amazing. My father and his old band got their instruments out and played all through the night. That helped my mother mellow a bit, and by the end of the night they were talking to each other, almost like a couple.

The next day I woke to an announcement. My father was going to take his responsibilities to his family seriously and soon we would all be united. However, that reunion was going to be in Wales, not France. It was not exactly what everyone had wanted to hear, but the main thing, it was said, was that our family would be together. So, however reluctantly, everyone agreed to do whatever they could to help us lay down some roots – including lending my father money if it was needed.

This time my father was true to his word. Within a few weeks the paperwork and travel documents had been completed and sent to us. We were moving to Wales. The penny had still not really dropped with me, but with everyone repeating, 'The main thing is that you're all together as a family,' after a while I came to believe it.

Our travel documents arrived with a note laying out a list of directions of how exactly to reach him. At the time he was still living in the choirmaster's spare room, in a small village called Abercynon at the head of the Cynon valley, where the Cynon river meets the Taff. That was going to be our home until we could afford something better. His instructions were very thorough. Jakub drove us to the station at Chalon-sur-Saone, where we caught a train to Paris Gard du Lyon. At Paris we had to get on a bus to get across the city to the Gard du Nord, then catch another train onto the Calais ferry terminal. We caught a ferry from Calais to Dover, and a train on to London. So far so good.

But things started to get a bit more complicated when we got to London Paddington. My father's directions were a little hazy on exactly which train we'd need to take us to Abercynon, and although neither my mother nor I had ever spoken a word of English in our lives, we found ourselves needing to ask a conductor for help. In her best pidgin English, my mother managed, 'Where is ze train for...' Then she paused. She couldn't speak English, let alone a Welsh placename! She tried her best and took another run at it. 'Where iz ze train for... A-ber-see-non.'

The conductor, a proper cockney, contracted his face into a tight, confused frown. 'What?' he asked.

'Ze train for A-ber-see-non...' my mother persisted.

He held out his hand, beckoning to look at the note she was reading from.

Taking it, he laughed out loud. 'Oh! You mean Aber-canyon!' (I was to find out soon enough that this was just as wrong as what my mother had said.) 'You wanna change at Cardiff, love. Platform six. In about twenty minutes.' She looked at him blankly. The glazed eyes told him that his instructions had not sunk in. He got out his pen and wrote a number six on my father's instructions and pointed in the general direction of the platform.

'Ah!' my mother said. 'Sssank you.' And off we trotted with our trolley teetering with suitcases and bags.

We arrived in Abercynon under the cover of night, so we could not really get much of an idea of our surroundings, and managed to struggle with all our bags to the house where my father lived. The door was opened by a warm, homely lady with a beaming smile, Mrs Elsie Jenkins. She was my father's landlady, the wife of Delwyn, the choirmaster, or 'Wyn-the-hymn' as he was known locally. She knew exactly who we were and immediately called her husband and my father to greet us and help us with our bags. She sat us by the fire, which was glowing in the grate, made us both a sandwich, my mother a cup of tea and me a mug of hot milk. It was so welcoming. My favourite memory of those early years in Wales was that first night with the Jenkinses. They had lost a son during the war. He had been killed in action while serving with the South Wales Board in North Africa, so now it was just the two of them. They had a photo of him in uniform on the mantelpiece, next to his medals mounted on a plaque. They were so kind and lovely. It seemed so unfair that they should be deprived of a son when they clearly must have made such loving parents. At least having a little girl in the house was something they could relish for a while. Mrs Jenkins put me in mind of my granny, so being around her in these strange new surroundings was good for me too.

The next day, I got to see Abercynon for the first time. It was something of a culture shock. As I think I have mentioned before, where we lived in France was quite a pretty little village. It had wide tree-lined streets, houses with big gardens, and we had woods, fields and countryside all around us. The sun frequently shone brightly in a pale blue sky, and the air was always full of birdsong and insects and colour.

The Cynon valley in 1948 could not have been further removed from that. There were houses and collieries everywhere, and the houses did not have gardens to the front. Your front door just opened straight onto the street. There did not seem to be any open spaces at all. It was the greyest place I had ever seen in my life. The sky, the houses and buildings, the roads, the streets, the trees, the rivers, even the complexions of the locals – everything everywhere was just different shades of grey. It was quite extraordinary. For someone artistic who loved colour and nature, it offered very little visually, and that is me being polite.

But I soon had other things to think about. I had been enrolled at the local school. I was by now ten years old, but I was unable to speak a word of English. To help me fit in, my parents did the same thing as when they'd enrolled me in a French school: they changed my name to Monica.

My schoolmates had all been told that a little French girl would be joining the class, and they were immediately suspicious. When I arrived that first morning, everyone stared at me like I had two heads. No one would talk to me, besides one of the grown-ups who was supposedly a French teacher. But woe betide anyone who learned the language from her: her French was abysmal. Then, out of the blue, one of the girls in my class plucked up the courage to speak to me. She had gone to the trouble of learning some French words to make me feel welcome.

'*Bonjour. Ca va*?' she said with a proud smile.

You could have knocked me down with a feather. I was so shocked to hear these familiar words that, from my facial expression, the other children in the class thought she must have said something shocking or obscene.

'Pay no attention to 'er,' one of them said, 'she's all chops.'

All chops or not, after that we became inseparable. Sheila Evans, her name was. Her father was a miner too, and he had fought in the war. She lived a few streets away from the Jenkins household. At first, I communicated with a lot of gesturing, and she would fill in the gaps for me in English. But as time went by, my vocabulary started to flourish.

Despite my new friend, I think it's fair to say that I hated moving to Wales. I was totally uprooted, leaving behind friends, family and a whole way of life – and for no good reason, as far as I could see anyway. The Jenkinses were lovely people, but my mother remained a bit of an odd fish at the best of times, and the more I got to know my father, the less I liked him. If I could have just jumped on a plane and gone back to France, I would have done so in a blink of an eye. I was terrified my French family and I might drift apart, and I wrote to my granny and uncles and aunts pretty much every day; when they wrote back, I would read their letters over and over again until I could visualise everything they told me, as if I was still there. Those letters meant so much to me. They were the only way I could maintain ties with my family and France; they were my escape, my happy place.

I had always been among the higher achieving kids in my school in France, so to suddenly have the handicap of not being able to speak the same language as my classmates was another thing I disliked. I had gone from being the teacher's pet to the class dunce overnight, and that did not sit comfortably with me at all. The thing that really lit a fuse under me, however, was a chat with my teacher at the start of the September term in what would be my final year of primary school. This was in the days when children had to sit their eleven plus exams. I really wanted to keep up my French, but I was told that, given my poor English, I would probably struggle to pass the eleven plus and would end up in a secondary modern, where French would not be an option. This was earth-shattering news to me. I had to make sure I passed those exams. I worked my little socks off on my English that year. The fact that my teachers had pretty much written me off just made me all the more determined to prove them wrong. I suppose if there was one positive thing I had inherited from my father, it was an obstinate determination to prove people wrong.

One year after arriving in the UK without the ability to say a single word in English, I passed my eleven plus. It turned out I could achieve things. I'd never known.

The Great Escape

Passing the eleven plus was a really big deal. No one had expected me to do it. My parents, my teachers, even my friend Sheila had all written me off. When I got my results and walked out of that school, it was with a grin a mile wide pasted across my face. Everyone's reaction put me in mind of when I'd survived diphtheria. They were all delighted and happy for me but, in equal measure, totally amazed. Which I have to say, I found a bit of a cheek. It's not as if I'd never displayed any signs of intelligence before. But from everyone's reaction, you would have sworn I'd always been a complete idiot. Even the local paper ran a piece on this little girl who had come over from France aged ten, and without knowing a word of English, in one year had gone on to get a place in Pontypridd Grammar School for Girls. Mrs Jenkins cut it out of the paper and hung it up on her wall. I thought that was brilliant.

The great thing about grammar school was that I was not 'the new girl' anymore. Everybody was new, and all from different schools. And not everybody came with their usual cohort of friends either, with some having gone to the secondary modern. Everybody was equally nervous, and everybody was quite open to the idea of making new friends and forming new social groups. By now my English was up to a standard where I could converse with pretty much anybody, so the language was no longer a barrier. At last I was starting to settle down and fit in.

As a family, we were also laying down some roots. My father had put us down for a council house, but we had not heard anything all year. Then one day we had a letter confirming that they were building a new wave of houses in Penyrheol near Caerphilly and that we were down to get one of those. That, we thought, was fantastic news. There was a bit of a mess up with dates, however. I'm not sure if it was my father's fault or the council's, but we gave our notice to the Jenkinses too early. The trouble was, by the time the mistake had been noticed, the Jenkins' nephew wanted to move in, to live closer to the mine where he worked. Our house was still not yet ready, so we had to find somewhere at very short notice to bridge the gap. We took lodgings at a house in Coedpenmaen, and oh my God, it was disgusting. The family who lived there were rough as old boots. They and their house stank to high heaven. Thankfully we were not there very long, just a few months, although even in that space of time I'd managed to catch both lice and rickets off them.

To get to our room, we had to walk through an adjoining room, which was let to another lodger. The toilet was down the hall, so we were constantly walking through his room, day and night, even when he was asleep in there. I remember one winter night when it was especially cold outside, into minus numbers, and the landlady became concerned for the welfare of her chickens in the garden. She let them into her kitchen so they could keep warm by the stove, but at some point they managed to escape and set off exploring their new surroundings. I will never forget heading off to our room to sleep, walking through the room next-door to ours, only to see the lodger sitting bolt upright in his bed looking decidedly uncomfortable. There was a row of chickens, huddled together for warmth, perched along the top of his bedstead, fast asleep. It was one of the funniest things I had ever seen.

Thankfully, by spring our house was ready. It wasn't one of the new houses, as we had thought, but a house is a house and this one was ours. We were all very house proud. My father was quite good with his hands, so he could always rise to decorating or simple carpentry and general remedial repairs around the house. My mother, meanwhile, had learned a lot about gardening from growing food during the war; she turned the small garden at the back of the house into a bounteous vegetable allotment in no time. She was also kept busy with work. Mrs Jenkins had introduced her to a lady who ran a laundry as well as undertaking alteration and seamstress work in Pontypridd. My mother did some occasional work for her, and because my mum was both very good at what she did and very cheap, the flow of work was quite regular. We were not exactly flush, but we had enough money coming in to get by.

My English was by far the best in the household, especially when it came to reading and writing, so any bills or official letters were handled by me. At eleven years old, I was the one who had to ensure that our rental payments were up to date, that our possessions were insured and things like that.

I am probably making it all sound a lot better than it was. I was bitterly unhappy. It wasn't that I especially disliked Wales. The place had started to grow on me. It's that life at home was awful and I could not see any way out from it.

My mother and father fought like cat and dog. It had been pretty bad when we'd lived with other people, but now we were behind closed doors in our own house, it soon got physical. My mother could never forgive my father for deserting her – not just for the Spanish Civil War, then the Second World War, but to cap it all off, for South Wales. She was certain that he had spent the whole war shagging his way across Europe; even now that we were all living together under the same roof, she was constantly accusing him of having women on the side. For his part, he had never wanted to be married to her. She was a bit dim, not much of a conversationalist, and her constant paranoia ground him down.

The rows soon came to follow a well-worn routine, inevitably spilling over into my father losing his rag and hitting her; then the next day, she would take her frustrations out on me, regardless of whether I had actually done anything wrong or not. She would re-enact everything she had ever seen her own father do when he had been at his worst, and there was nothing I could do about it. It continued throughout my teenage years. The only time we ever spent together, the only bonding we ever did, was when she was overrun with seamstress and tailoring work. Then she would sit me down and instruct me on what needed doing. Because I had been helping since I was tiny, I already had a good idea of what I needed to do, and we would work side by side, taking turns on her sewing machine.

My relationship with my father was no better. As he had never known me as a small child, he had no paternal instincts towards me whatsoever. I was just some girl living in his house. When I hit puberty and started to develop breasts and a figure, the way he used to leer at me was just plain creepy. And what is worse, when my mother spotted it, rather than leap to my defence and protect me, she started to treat me as if I was 'the other woman'. I mean, how messed up can you get?

There was no Childline or refuge or any kind of instant access to social services that I knew about back then. If you were abused at home, then tough. You just had to put up with it. At least in France I could have diluted my mother with other members of the family. Here I was trapped 24/7. In my most desperate moments, I used to cry myself to sleep at night. I felt abandoned and betrayed. I felt angry.

I had been brought up to be good Catholic girl, but where the hell was God now? Where was he now I needed him? Why was he letting this happen to me? Why were the very people meant to protect me and keep me safe inflicting all this pain? In my darkness and despair, I lost my faith and never got it back. I wanted to be able to draw the same strength from it that my granny got. But I just couldn't. And I felt guilty about that, which of course just made the situation worse again.

I snatched at any opportunity I could find to get out of the house. I took on two paper rounds, and signed up for every after-school activity that you didn't have to pay for. I joined the choir and the orchestra and the gymnastics troupe. Every single Saturday morning, without fail, Sheila Evans and I would go to the cinema for the matinees. We saw every film that came out, and I relished losing myself in the glamour of it all for a couple of hours.

Schoolwork was an escape as well. I threw myself totally into my studies. When I was home, I would lock myself in my room and make my homework last as long as I could. I breezed through my O Levels, getting ten A grades, one B grade and a C grade. I even got an A in Welsh. The C was in Polish! They didn't do Polish as a subject at my school, but as I had been speaking it with my family since I was a baby, it was worth taking the exam. The C grade gives you an idea of the quality of the language spoken in my home. Until then I hadn't realised it, but it was full of the slang and colloquialisms of everyday speech; I was quite lucky to come away with a C, if I'm honest.

It was in the sixth form that I realised that my best route out from under my parents' roof was academia. If I could just get into a university, preferably one too far away for me to live at home, then happy days. I'd be gone, and my parents wouldn't be able to make my life a misery anymore. For whatever reason, they threw every obstacle they could in my path to stop me. Why? I don't know. It's not as if they seemed to get any pleasure from having me around. I think they just hated the idea that I might ever be happy or be independent of them.

But I was determined. My A Level predictions were good enough for me to apply pretty well anywhere, and I had set my heart on Bristol. It was far enough away that I would have to leave home, but close enough for me to maintain contact with my friends, plus it was a really good university, and I had been to Bristol twice and really liked it. My parents, however, refused to help me with the train fare to attend my interview. This incident, though cruel, crystalised in my mind how manipulative my parents were capable of being and strengthened my resolve not to rely on them for anything. From then on, if I had an interview anywhere, I would save up my paper round money to attend it. I left the house every Saturday morning, so my parents would think I was still spending my money on the cinema as usual, and if I ever needed a top up, Sheila always came up trumps. I had a very good interviews at King's College London and also at Exeter, and I would have been happy with either. I messed up a bit at Imperial College London, though, so I knew that would not go any further. I also did well at my interview with Cardiff, although I had sort of written this off as I was concerned it might be too close to Caerphilly.

I ended up getting Four As at A Level, which was good enough to enter any of these great institutions to study Modern Languages – French more specifically, with a view to going on to do teacher training and becoming a French teacher.

Drawing on my experience with the household paperwork, I did my own grant application, which only took account of my father's income as a miner. I didn't see the need to mention my mother's income as a seamstress, as it was all cash in hand work, which I'm sure she didn't want made public, and it might have scuppered my chances of getting a full grant. I was probably far better prepared for this element of student life than most of my age group. I knew exactly what it cost to run a household, as I saw all our bank statements, and a quick glance at the figures told me that, even with a full grant, it was going to be a real struggle to make ends meet if I moved out (which was the whole point).

Then quite by chance a teacher at my school asked me if I had been successful in my application for a bursary. 'What's a bursary?' I asked. It turned out there was a specific fund set up by the miner's union to support the children of South Wales miners who got a place at university. It was a way of improving social mobility amongst its members. She just assumed I'd know about it through my father. I got in touch with the union, and sure enough, the bursary did exist, although it was only available if you attended a Welsh university. So that decided it: Cardiff here I come.

I didn't tell my parents that I had confirmed my place at university until the day before I planned to leave. It was a Sunday. They were furious, as I had predicted they would be, but I knew full well they both had work commitments the following day, so that night I packed my suitcases while everyone was asleep, and by the time they got up to go to work, I was walking out through the front door, ready to catch the first bus into Cardiff. Everyone else on the bus was commuting to work, but I was starting a whole new life, away from my parents, away from the pain, the constant humiliation, the control and the manipulation. I sat back in my seat, huddling my cluster of bags and cases close to me, a proud smile fixed to my lips.

The advantage of having Cardiff so close was that I could go down the week before I left home and do all the groundwork in preparation for the start of term. To maintain distance from my parents, though, I did not tell them what my new address was. It was inevitable that they would find out at some point, but I figured that once I was in my new accommodation, there would be nothing they could do about it. I had a lot more riding on my success at university than most of my peers. It made me all the more determined to make it work.

Despite my impeccable planning, though, I was always a bit nervous that I might run out of money. I had the grant, I had the bursary, all of which should have been enough to see me through term, but to make sure I wouldn't need to leave Cardiff even during the holidays, I took a leaf out of my mother's book and went to visit a shop which offered tailoring, alterations and clothing repairs, and offered them my services. It was a very old fashioned little shop, upstairs in the Castle Arcade in Cardiff. It was owned by a Polish-born Jew called Mr Epstein. He had fled Warsaw when the Nazis first invaded Poland and had made a new life for his family in Cardiff. He ran the shop with his son, Saul. They were both so old fashioned, like they had stepped out of a Dickens novel. Mr Epstein wore half-spectacles which he kept on a leash around his neck. When he talked to you, he would peer over the top of them. He always wore the same black pinstripe, three-piece suit, with a gold chain hung across his waistcoat attached to a pocket watch. He had thin wispy white hair and a big bushy beard. His son, Saul, was probably only in his early thirties or late twenties, but he had the demeanour of someone in his fifties. He was quietly spoken, tall and so painfully thin he looked like a toothpick. He was always immaculately dressed, his jet black, Brylcreemed hair tightly combed back off his forehead. I did a little demonstration for the two of them so they could see what I was capable of, and they examined my needlework very closely. Mr Epstein senior looked up at me and gave an appreciative smile, eyebrows raised over the rim of his glasses. He offered me work every Saturday. I'm not sure what my Mum would have made of it: utilising the one skill she had imparted to me to put as much distance between us as possible.

Right from the start and throughout my first term, I knuckled down really hard on my course. After a month or two my parents somehow managed to find out what my address was, but as I said, I'd known that this was inevitable at some point. They wrote to me asking me to come home for Christmas, saying that they were sorry if I felt they had pushed me away or behaved poorly towards me. This was the closest I had ever come to an apology, but I wasn't ready to go back just yet, not even for a one day visit. In the back of my mind, rightly or wrongly, I suspected that if I was to go home they might do something drastic like lock me in a bedroom or something like that, to prevent me from returning to university. That may have been a legitimate fear, it may have been paranoia. But do you know what? I was in no hurry to find out which.

I did, however, write back, confirming that I did indeed feel that they had treated me very badly and confirming that, owing to the beatings and the nonsense I had put up with over the years, I was in no hurry to come home for anything. But I agreed that, after Christmas, if they still wanted to, I would be prepared to meet them somewhere in Cardiff. I made it clear, though, that I did not feel safe going back to their house. Not yet.

And that is what happened. When the first term ended for the Christmas break, I stayed on in halls. I got a job at David Morgan, the up-market department store in the Hayes, where I got my first experience of working in fashion retail. I was making and mending clothes on a Saturday for Mr Epstein, and from Monday to Friday I was selling them to wealthy ladies in David Morgan. It all came quite naturally to me. I seemed to get on with my customers, and they got on with me. I even had some regulars who would ask for me when they arrived, and who bought me little gifts when the Christmas break ended and I was to go back to university.

Christmas day itself was a bit weird. I had gone out on Christmas Eve with a bunch of girls from David Morgan and had got quite drunk, so on Christmas Day I slept in until late. I got up and made myself some breakfast (even though it was lunchtime) and then I went for a walk. It was a cold, drizzly day and the air was filled with that saturating rain that gets into everything. But I had a good winter coat on, so I walked around the municipal buildings of Cathays Park in the centre of Cardiff. Normally they were a hive of activity, buzzing with cars and people. But on Christmas day, it was completely silent and deserted, like some post-apocalyptic parallel universe. I quite enjoyed the silence, a moment of selfish, blissful melancholy all to myself.

I had made a handful of friends in that first term, but socialising wasn't that high a priority for me. The best friend I had made was a girl called Barbara, who everyone knew as Babs. She was quite posh, about the same age as me (give or take a few months) and as such was also in her first year. She studied Fine Art and she lived in the room opposite me in our halls. She had quite a large social group and frequently threw parties both at halls and occasionally at her parents' house.

She usually invited me to come along but I did not indulge myself in much socialising at this point of my university career. But after several polite refusals and in a week when I felt suitably on top of my studies, I agreed. I told Mr Epstein of my plans.

'Good,' he said. 'It doesn't do for a girl of your age to work so much'. He told me to go along, and maybe I would meet some nice young man. Nothing could have been further from my thoughts.

On the Friday afternoon, Babs and I caught the train to her parents' house in Radyr, a rather well-to-do village on the outskirts of Cardiff. We walked the final stage of the journey to the house. High walls screened the houses on our side of the pavement from sight, and as we reached a driveway, Babs suddenly stopped.

'This is us,' she declared, leading me up the driveway to a vast house. I checked myself. I *had* seen bigger houses: the chateau at Blanzy, for example, where Aunty Nadia had worked was much bigger. But that was pretty much it, and I had never entered there as a guest.

We walked in through the front door, Babs calling out loudly to her parents, announcing our arrival. Part of me wanted to sink through the floor before anyone saw me. Not only was this place huge, but it was so beautifully decorated and furnished. Huge chandeliers hung, sparkling, from the high vaulted ceiling in the hall, the tiled floor washing up to the foot of a sweeping castellated staircase. Old paintings hung in clusters on the walls, and all around the perimeter of every room were elegant antique furnishings and displays.

Barbara's family and friends were all nice enough, very polite and easy to talk to. But it was all a bit of a culture shock to me. I had never met truly posh people before. My only idea of them was from reading *Billy Bunter* stories. I was rather intimidated and overwrought. I hardly said a word all weekend.

Amongst the revellers in Radyr was a slightly larger than life character. His name was James but he went by Jim. He was a first-year law student at Cardiff who had been brought up by a great aunt living in Wales after being evacuated from his parents' house in London during the war. They, I was to find out later, were the most terrible snobs and social climbers, and at the time, he can't have been that different from them, as he came to the party dressed like Noel Coward, complete with silk cravat and long cigarette holder. But as the evening wore on, he put his flamboyance to one side and sat next to me and just talked. Underneath the affectations he was very sweet. He could see I was out on the periphery a bit, so he went out of his way to talk to me and make me feel welcome. We had a bit in common too. We both loved films, and also he was a bit of a Francophile. He was fascinated with where I had come from. It came as no surprise to me that he had never heard of Montceau-les-Mines, but he took me to the library in the house to dig up an atlas so I could show him on the map where I had grown up.

I hadn't had a lot of experience of boys and was rather naive, young for my age in that respect. I didn't pick up on those clues that Babs had, and which she detailed to me in breathy excitement. Jim, it seemed, was quite sweet on me. If she was right, then I didn't think it was a bad thing. He was good company, witty, intelligent, easy to talk to and quite good looking in his way. He presented himself very much in the mould of an English gentleman of means. He wore stripey blazers and flannel, often with a cricket sweater knotted around his waist, and he spoke very confidently. He was also cultured, unlike most of the people I had known since coming to Wales. He knew and loved French composers like Emile Saint-Sans, Eric Satie and Claude Debussy. Besides the music teacher at Pontypridd Grammar, and our former landlord and choirmaster, Mr Jenkins, no one else I knew in Wales had ever even heard of them.

In the weeks that followed, even though I had never seen him visit Babs before, Jim contrived to bump into me at halls several times. Quite soon, he plucked up the courage to ask me out to dinner. It was the start of my first proper relationship. But there was still another relationship in my life that I needed to address.

When I finally agreed to meet my parents for the first time since moving out, it was towards the latter part of the spring term. We agreed to meet in a café by the boating lake at Roath Park, just round the corner from where Jim lived. But even though he and I had been out together a few times at that point, I had decided not to mention him yet. One thing at a time.

I arrived at the café first. When my mother saw me sitting there all grown up and independent, she burst into tears, running up to me and holding me in the tightest embrace I had ever received from her. She wept into my neck. I held my arms out to her but could not bring myself to hug her back. My father was very sheepish. He didn't say much, only to tell me how much my mother had been missing me, and how my mother wanted to see more of me and how much she loved me.

Despite everything, I believed him: in her own way, I think she genuinely did love me, only that she was rubbish at showing it. I think he loved me too, in his own way. And I knew I loved them, but that did not mean that I was prepared to undo all that I had done to get away from them. We agreed to meet in Cardiff once a month after that – sometimes just my mum, sometimes both of them – and that seemed to work OK for everyone.

By the end of the summer term, Jim and I had been going steady, but I was to discover that he was never short of surprises. Despite finishing year one of his law degree studies top of his year, he had been sacked off his course. It was discovered that in his university application he had lied about having passed his Maths O Level. These days, with everything computerised, that would not be possible, but back then, if you were brazen enough to try, there was every possibility you might get away with it. At least that was his justification. Suffice it to say he was suddenly no longer enlisted at the university. I was only just starting my second year.

His original plan was to do the rest of his course by correspondence, but he wanted us to move in together while he did. I think I panicked at this suggestion. I really was not ready for such a big commitment. So I told him no. Having only just won my freedom from my parents, I wasn't yet ready to relinquish it. He really was not happy about this and threw a rather childish tantrum about the whole thing. He said if I didn't want to live with him, then I didn't want to be with him at all. And if that was the case, he declared, we should split up. Rather coldly, I agreed with him. So that's what we did. He moved back in with his great aunt to continue his studies, and I stayed in halls. In the days after, I cried and cried. I did love him. And I didn't agree to a split because I had any other prospects. It's just that I wasn't ready for that chapter in my life just yet.

I finished top of my year in both year one and year two of my degree. In my final year, those of us who were doing our language degree with an intention to go into teaching had the opportunity to undertake a three-month placement in a French school. I volunteered as quick as a flash; one of the schools we could volunteer for was the Lycée at Macon, an hour's bus drive from my family in Les Baudrats. It was the first opportunity I'd had to go back and see them since leaving home. Not to mention, this way I could go without my parents and have an honest conversation with my granny about what had happened since we had left France. As the placement was for a few months, I could also stay with them, spend some real quality time with all of them, and pocket the allowance for my accommodation. It was like a dream come true.

My placement could not come around fast enough, but finally, on a freezing January morning, I boarded a train from Cardiff and travelled to Dover. I stayed the night in a cold and drafty B&B near the port, a tall, old, Edwardian house, probably quite grand in its heyday, but more than a little run down by now. I remember that the heavy front door had some kind of brass draft excluder around it which sung like a reed whenever the wind blew through. It was a very flat, ominous tone, and it kept me awake most of the night. Not that I could have slept a wink anyway. In the morning I would be boarding a ferry for France, and I was brimming with excitement at that prospect.

Being back with my family was every bit as brilliant as I'd hoped it would be. I stayed with my granny in the house I'd grown up in at Les Baudrats. Even though she was old, she was still tough as old boots, and she was glad of the company, as she was now living there on her own. Michiek had finally moved out and got a place of his own (although he was still single) and Zarec had died in the years after the war (no great loss there). Aunty Anetka, meanwhile, had left the region completely. She was now residing in Paris, had found a man and settled down with him, and they were living a pseudo-Bohemian existence together, running a café to subsidise his real passion, which was acting. They were permanently broke because he kept taking acting jobs in plays that no one wanted to see, while she worked herself to the bone in the café. Every now and then they would have a massive row, and she would come back to stay with my granny for a few weeks, and then he would arrive in his rather beaten-up old Citroen and take her back home again.

Pawel and Nadia were both in fine form, and their son Lukasz, only a baby when I had left to start my new life in Wales, was now in his teens. He and I really hit it off. For those months I was in France he was like a little brother to me. He also now had a younger sister, Magda, who was eight. It was amazing to think that this was the first time I had ever met her. Jakub and Mira were also both doing well, although Jakub had been struggling with his respiration. As he was a miner, his doctor had recommended him to a specialist in case it was dust on the lung. When the specialist saw him, he recognised Jakub instantly; he was a massive Gueugnon Football Club fan, and here he was treating one of the heroes of 1947. He was completely starstruck. The two of them spent the hour that had been allocated for examination reliving the 1947 season match by match. At the end of the session they shook hands, and Jakub asked, 'Aren't you going to examine me?'

The specialist shook his head. 'Don't you worry about that,' he said.

Within a month, Jakub had the test results come back. Without even examining him, this specialist had signed him off with 100% dust. As a result, Jakub had a huge compensation pay out and received an early pension from the pit. As soon as he was retired off, he and Mira and Alinka spent a month in the south of France, and on his return, he started a new job as a fireman. They were living a good life. Their daughter Alinka wanted for nothing.

Less happily, I told my granny all about my life growing up with my parents. She wept and held me close, stroking my head, and I wept too. It was really cathartic. In the back of her mind, she had known it was a possibility, having seen how my mother had behaved towards me when I was younger, but she had hoped against hope things would be better when we were reunited with my father. She took me to Mass the next day so we could pray for a path of peace with my parents. I didn't have the heart to tell her that I had lost my faith, and to be honest, I was just so happy to be kneeling at her side again, clutching my rosary in that echoey little church. To this day, if I ever hear Mass, it always transports me back to that time, and I weep with all my heart.

Between my placement and spending time with my family, I kept up a weekly correspondence with my friends back home, including Babs. Then one morning I had a letter from Jim. When I saw the envelope, I recognised the handwriting instantly. Babs must have passed him my granny's address from a letter I had sent her. It wasn't a love letter as such. There was no poetry (although he did consider himself a bit of a poet) nor any declarations of undying love. It was just an enquiry about how I was. What was it like being back in France? He also provided an update on what he was up to back in Wales, and how his studies were going. I wrote back in similar terms and so we started corresponding.

'Can I come over to see you?' he asked in his third letter.

'Yes, of course,' I replied. 'Shall I ask my granny if you can stay here, or did you have somewhere else in mind?'

'If I could stay with your granny, that would be fantastic,' came his response. So I told her all about Jim, about how we had grown close, about how I had effectively pushed him away, and how he had now got in touch and asked if he could stay.

'Of course! Of course he can,' she said excitedly. 'I would love to meet him.'

And so it was that Jim came to stay with us for a week. I showed him around where I had grown up, as well as Macon and the school where I was teaching. We ate lunch at my favourite restaurant on the banks of the river, at St Laurent-sur-Saone looking back over the bridge at the old city. And after that, we walked along the banks of the Saone holding hands. We stopped and sat under a tree, where we finished off a bottle of wine we had started with our lunch, talking, laughing, and flicking stones into the river. And then we watched the sun set before we caught the last bus home, which wound its way through the vineyards of the Macconaise, through the historic town of Cluny with its vast abbey, and onto Montceau and home. It was quite magical.

He met every member of my extended family before he ever met my parents, and they all loved him. And he seemed to love them too. And as for me, I think I had always loved him. It was only that, two years earlier, my head had been in the wrong place to realise it.

Allo! Allo! Ici Londres

I graduated from Cardiff with a really solid upper second, which I should have been more happy with than I was at the time. Jim and I had been an item since his visit to France in the spring term, but as I approached my finals, he gave me the space I needed to commit to my studies. He continued to live with his aunt without making any demands, and every couple of weeks he would come to Cardiff to see me, and we would spend some time together. I would write to him most days, and he would respond with similar regularity. It was no surprise to anyone when, after my exams were over, the two of us moved in together, into a little rooftop flat in Llandaff.

Despite the disgrace of being kicked out of university, Jim had gone on to qualify as a solicitor and was earning good money for someone of his age, working for a very successful but traditional law firm with offices in the centre of Cardiff. I had soon started teacher training, and throughout that year we lived an enjoyable, albeit bohemian, life.

But while from the outside everything might have seemed like it was coming together, I was beginning to falter over whether I truly wanted to go into teaching. When I qualified, I was unable to find a placement in a Cardiff school, so I ended up teaching in a school near Bridgend – which ironically was only a few miles from where Jim had been living with his great aunt.

I could not put off introducing Jim to my parents any longer. I had told them about him in letters, and in conversations when we would have our little meetings in person, but I had not given away how serious it was. I had also spoken to Jim about my troubled history with my parents and how I had disowned them, but I had never gone into the details. But now there was nothing for it but to arrange a visit to the house in Caerphilly. It was rather an awkward meeting. Jim was his usual charming, polite self, but my parents were guarded to say the least. I was a bag of nerves and hated every second of it.

When I met his parents, it was no different. They were very suspicious of me. I suppose they thought that this miner's daughter from Caerphilly was some kind of gold-digger, sniffing around Jim for his money. That was a bit of cheek. Yes, they had a bit of money and some clear middle class credentials, but they were not exactly high rollers. Jim's father (also called Jim!) was a talented scientist and something of an entrepreneur. He was undoubtedly very intelligent and had patented a type of washing detergent which his own company produced in a small factory in east London. It made them a perfectly decent living, enough for Jim's mother not to need to work, and they had a perfectly decent flat, but they were such terrible snobs that they liked to create the impression they were a lot more than 'perfectly decent'. For one thing, they did the classic London social climbers' trick of pretending to live in a much more affluent address than they really occupied. There was absolutely nothing wrong with where they *did* live, yet they would insist they lived in Hurlingham, a very exclusive address on the river in southwest London. In reality, they lived just off Fulham High Street. Fulham, of course, is very desirable these days, but back then it was considered a bit duergar by the middle classes. The most ridiculous thing was that they kept up this pretence even to me. I had never heard of either Fulham or Hurlingham until I met them. I could not have cared less.

They had clearly hoped that their son would marry someone more upper middle class, like Babs, to give them an extra foothold on the social ladder. But alas, that is not something I could help them with. Both of these meetings, with both set of our parents, were pretty disastrous for opposite sides of the same reason. But the clear lack of approval from both sets of our parents just made us more convinced that being together was the right thing. Stuff the lot of them. Let's get married!

Those early years were some of the happiest of my life. I was married to a man I loved and who worshipped me; I loved my work, he loved his; we had great social lives together and the world seemed to be our oyster. It wasn't perfect, of course. For one thing, I still had to spell out my surname! All of my life, I had had to spell out 'Kowolska' whenever I was asked it, and I had long looked forward to the day when I might marry a local and have a surname people knew. And then I went and married someone called 'Devilliers'!

But what really nagged me was my career. As much as I loved my job, when I looked to the future, I just could not see myself as a teacher.

All my life I had been interested in clothes and fashion. The regular trips I now made to southwest London to visit Jim's parents inevitably meant a jaunt down the nearby Kings Road, to visit the likes of Mary Quant and the other pillars of London fashion that were down there. And the more often I visited, the more I realised that there was no outlet for this sort of stuff in South Wales. And surely, with the sixties being in full swing, there was a demand for it.

It wasn't lost on me that I could design clothes, makes clothes, sell clothes, and that I had customers who knew me by name from when I had worked in David Morgan. Jim was very supportive, and he was great when it came to the financial stuff like business planning and things like that, and to be fair, I was pretty good with numbers too. But it was the money to get off the ground that I lacked, not to mention the contacts.

Help, however, came from all sorts of unforeseen places. Firstly, my old school friend Sheila came up trumps, introducing me to the fashion writer for *The Sunday Times*. This was a very flamboyant bon viveur called Molly Parkin. She was a major player and knew everything about the London fashion scene and everyone in it. And of all places, she was originally from the Garw Valley. She had grown up a few streets away from Sheila's mum, and she had gone to the same schools as a few people I knew from teaching. You would never have known it if you met her, though. She was all 'lovey' and 'darling' when she spoke. In the time she had been away, she had become far more Pimlico than Pant-y-Gog.

Sheila's mother was a very good friend of Mrs Parkin, Molly's mother, and had known Molly since she was a tiny baby. So, when I told her about my ambitions, Sheila tapped into the 'Welsh Mam's Network' and arranged an introduction.

'She'd be happy to help and she's waiting for your call!' she said excitedly, when we caught up on the phone. So the next day I phoned the offices of *The Sunday Times*, spoke to Molly (mainly about people and teachers and places we had in common) and made an appointment to meet up at her office.

She was so helpful. She gave me the inside track on so many things and introduced me to some fantastic contacts. I honestly don't think I could ever have got my business off the ground without her advice and help. We remained firm friends for many years.

Further help came from a truly unexpected source, someone who could not have surprised me more: Jim Devilliers senior, my father-in-law.

As frosty as he may have been towards me at first, I think he liked the idea of someone else in the family having some entrepreneurial spirit. I think that the glamour of the fashion industry appealed to him too. Having a hand in a top fashion outlet would probably provide good story value at dinner parties. He did all the usual networking, working the Freemasons and the Rotary Club, and through one of these organisations tapped up a friend who owned and rented out several shops, including one which was currently empty, slap bang in the centre of Bridgend, opposite the town hall. Thanks to Jim's dad we got this shop in a fantastic location and with very favourable terms. Jim's dad also lent us some money to get ourselves started, as neither me nor Jim had any collateral to borrow from a bank. Things were tough at first, as they always are with a new business, and I had to work very hard for a lot of hours for very little return. But by the second year we started making a bit of money – with fortunate timing, because in that second year, Jim's father's business collapsed, and my paying him back got him out of a tough spot.

The collapse came about largely because he had not been supervising things properly. As I said before, Jim's parents liked to give the impression that they were people of leisure, so every opportunity they had, they would go swanning off to Menton on the Cote d'Azur, leaving a rather junior and inexperienced manager in charge at the factory. One day when they were away, he got the recipe for their washing detergent wrong, and a whole batch went out that was so concentrated that any clothes washed in it were disintegrated and skin exposed to it burned. A class action of claimants was brought in the county court, suing the company as a result of damaged property and injury. The claim was upheld and the damages awarded were so huge that it forced the company into liquidation. Just like that, my father-in-law was ruined. They had to sell the flat in London to cover their debts and moved to a modest house owned by Jim's mother's family.

I felt really sorry for them. Losing everything like that would be hard on anyone, but for a couple who put so much stock in what other people thought, it must have been mortifying. Still, my loan repayments at least gave them some kind of income while he sorted out his affairs, and they didn't stay down and out for long. As a qualified pharmacist, my father-in-law didn't have any difficulty getting a job. Initially he managed a branch of an independent pharmacy chain in Bridgend, while Jim's mother went back into teaching. Within a couple of years, they had their own shop in Tonypandy, in the Rhondda Valley, and the two of them were earning enough to get themselves back into a rather comfortable standard of living. They had fallen some distance from the life they had been living, but nonetheless had a very comfortable lifestyle by most comparisons.

Since I had first hatched my plan to get away from my parents as a teenager, I had been very focussed on being in control of my life: on always having a plan, a contingency. And it was working: here I was, happily married to the man of my choosing, my own boss, with a promising business and the world at my feet. Then there came a bolt from the blue.

I was pregnant.

I had every reason to be delighted with this news. My life was going well, I was settled down in my own home with a man who adored me, and I knew that Jim would be over the moon. But the news hit me like I'd been punched in the stomach. I was terrified that the way my grandfather and mother had treated their children was somehow genetic; that I was doomed to be a rubbish parent, a bully and an abuser. For the same reasons, given how inappropriately my father had behaved towards me, if I were to have a daughter, I was terrified I would never be able to trust Jim around a little girl. That I would have to explain to Jim why. That was a conversation I did not want to have. I felt sick. This news, which should have been the best news ever, was eating away at me. It was not until after I had missed three periods that I told Jim. By then I'd had time to practise being delighted in case it did not come naturally to me.

The pregnancy went smoothly, and I spent the months leading up to the birth doing all the usual things, nesting around our flat, plus making sure the shop was staffed up to run without me for six months (and not to make the same mistake as Jim's dad). I could not bring myself to tell my parents face to face that I was pregnant, so I wrote them a letter instead. I also wrote to everyone in France, an altogether more enjoyable letter to write. Everyone wrote back. The doormat was awash with envelopes with Montceau postmarks. I read them all one by one and really wished my granny could be with me through it all.

As much as nothing could have prepared me for the shock of falling pregnant, equally, nothing could have prepared me for the sheer ecstasy and pride which overcame me when I held my newborn baby son for the first time. Every fear just drained away. And when Jim was allowed in to see us in the hospital for the first time, we both just burst into tears in each other's arms. None of this had been part of any plan, but it was the best thing that had ever happened to me.

'Where am I from?' I knew the answer to that, even though there was no quick way to say it. 'Where was I going?' Not a clue. But I was so looking forward to finding out.